THE PICTURE BOX

A HISTORICAL MYSTERY

FROM AN ORIGINAL STORY BY
DARIO DIMITRIC AND CARLO ARMENISE

Carlo Armenise

Author's Tranquility Press
ATLANTA, GEORGIA

Copyright © 2023 by Carlo Armenise

All rights reserved. No part of this publication may be reproduced, distributed or transmitted in any form or by any means, including photocopying, recording, or other electronic or mechanical methods, without the prior written permission of the publisher, except in the case of brief quotations embodied in critical reviews and certain other noncommercial uses permitted by copyright law. For permission requests, write to the publisher, addressed "Attention: Permissions Coordinator," at the address below.

The Picture Box/Author's Tranquility Press
3800 Camp Creek Pkwy SW Bldg. 1400-116 #1255
Atlanta, GA 30331, USA
www.authorstranquilitypress.com

Ordering Information:
Quantity sales. Special discounts are available on quantity purchases by corporations, associations, and others. For details, contact the "Special Sales Department" at the address above.

The Picture Box/Carlo Armenise
Paperback: 978-1-962859-04-2
eBook: 978-1-962492-94-2

Several real historical characters, places, and events appear on the pages of this book, while pieces of the story are fictional.

CONTENTS

Chapter I 1

Chapter II 16

Chapter III 37

Chapter IV 50

Chapter V 62

Chapter VI 76

Chapter VII 86

CHAPTER I

Dreams, the stories the mind tells during certain stages of sleep, are believed to be the result of reliving life experiences. Some dreams bring back memories of joy and happiness, while others replay sadness and loss. For thirty-six-year-old Dario Dimitric, born in Osijek, Croatia, his dreams always brought back memories of the homeland he left behind.

Bordered on one side by the Adriatic Sea, Croatia is part of Southeastern Europe and one of the world's most beautiful countries. But despite its' baroque charm, Croatia is no stranger to conflict. In 1991, after years of being under the supervision of the communist Socialist Federal Republic of Yugoslavia, Croatia wanted its independence from communism and went to war with Yugoslavia to regain control of its borders and establish an independent state that only allowed Catholic Croatians.

Before the war, Croatia had a multi-ethnic, multi-religious population comprised of Croats, Serbians, Jews, and Gypsies, and mixed marriages were commonplace. In fact, Dario's mother, Blanka, was Croatian, and his father, Nikola, was Serbian.

The Picture Box

In order to increase the size of their army for the war, the Croatian government required all the non-Croatians living in the country to either renounce their original ethnicity and fight for Croatia or leave the country.

Dario's father refused to reject his Serbian heritage, and he and Dario's mother left Croatia and moved to France. At the same time, Dario stayed in Osijek and moved in with his Croatian grandmother, Ljubica Kvaternik, to finish his final college semester before joining his parents.

Since Ljubica disapproved of her daughter marrying a Serbian, and especially one she felt was a malcontent, Dario didn't see her very often growing up. And besides knowing that his seventy-five-year-old grandmother's family name, Kvaternik, was a part of Croatian history and that she was wealthy, the rest of her life was a mystery to Dario.

After he moved in with her, Dario discovered his grandmother was a highly respected woman in Osijek with unquestionable integrity, character, and generosity. Besides overcoming the adversities of World War Two and protecting her family, she was also the first woman in Osijek to have a driver's license and was the one-time owner of the Hotel Royal, still a famous Croatian landmark.

Inspired by his grandmother's achievements, Dario focused on developing his talent as a singer with a goal to one day go to America and become famous. An idea his grandmother supported and encouraged, especially considering the political climate in Croatia. Dario's musical talent came from his father's side of the family. His grandfather, Stanko, was a well-known Serbian violin player who Ljubica knew of and admired long before their son and daughter met and married. And even though the Croatians rebuffed Stanko because of his heritage, Ljubica would have him play at the Royal, welcoming the attention his talent brought to the hotel.

As the war started, Dario, like all the other Croatian men, was ordered to join the army and fight. However, because of his mixed heritage, Dario decided he couldn't support the war and prepared to join his parents in France. But before Dario could leave Osijek, he got the life-changing news his parents were killed in a car accident.

Traumatized by his parents' death and trying to cope with life's uncertainty without them, Dario became depressed and withdrawn and stopped singing. And Ljubica, knowing she would never see her daughter again to tell her how much she loved her, no matter their differences, suffered overwhelming sorrow.

As Ljubica and Dario tried to cope with the situation, they consoled one another and grew close. Dario came to rely on his grandmother for the love and support he once got from his parents, and Ljubica came to see Dario as a son and a wonderful reminder of her daughter.

After his parents' funeral, Ljubica, still supporting Dario's decision not to fight in the war, used her government connections and got him a visa that allowed him to go to America to pursue his singing.

"I don't know how I'll ever be able to repay you, Grandmother," Dario said.

"You can repay me by following your dream and becoming a famous singer. And promise to come back to Osijek to see me when you can."

"I will. I love you," Dario replied.

With Ljubica's financial support, Dario left Osijek and went to America to a Croatian community his grandmother knew of in Miami and found work waiting tables and singing at a Croatian restaurant - all the while staying in touch with his grandmother and sharing his experiences.

"I'm getting noticed singing in Miami, Grandmother. I know I'll find success in America."

"I knew you would, Grandson. I'm so proud of you."

"Thank you for believing in me."

Dario quickly built a reputation as a talented entertainer, and one night a distinguished-looking sixty-year-old man came into the restaurant and heard him sing.

"My name is Harold Kingston and I own a nightclub in Denver, Colorado. Would you consider coming to Denver and performing at my club? I have a large, international clientele that I know will love you and make us both a lot of money."

Deciding he was ready to leave Miami and thrilled by the opportunity to sing for an international audience, Dario accepted and shared his good fortune with his grandmother.

"I was offered a singing job at an international nightclub in Denver, Colorado," Dario said.

"Congratulations, Grandson."

"But I miss you and Osijek. How is it there since the war?"

"It's not the same. A lot of people either left the country or got killed in the war."

"I'm worried about you, Grandmother. I feel guilty that I didn't stay in Osijek and take care of you."

"Don't worry about me, I'm fine. Just keep pursuing your dream and be well."

"You, too. I'll call you when I get to Denver."

Dario moved to Denver and was an immediate success. But after a few years, he recognized Denver wasn't going to take his career any further, and he entered an international singing competition and won a contract to headline a lounge act in Las Vegas. Thrilled, Dario called his grandmother, now eighty-five, and told her the good news.

"I'm going to Las Vegas to star in my own show, Grandmother."

"That's fantastic, Grandson, but please don't let Las Vegas turn you into a gambler like your uncle Philip."

"Don't worry, it won't."

Philip was Ljubica's and her first husband, Pero Truntic's son, and Blanka's older brother. When Philip was twelve and Blanka was ten, Ljubica and Pero, a Nazi sympathizer during World War Two, divorced. Pero moved to Frankfurt, Germany, and took Philip with him, while Blanka stayed in Osijek with Ljubica.

Not understanding why he was being separated from his mother and sister and forced to leave his friends and the life he loved in Osijek, Philip became despondent and angry. He felt abandoned by his mother and thought it was because she loved his sister more than she loved him. And even though Ljubica assured him it wasn't true, Philip didn't believe it and stopped speaking to her.

When Philip got to Frankfurt, he had trouble adjusting. Living in a strange city without friends and not knowing the German language, he felt isolated and alone. Even though Pero did what he could to help Philip acclimate, Pero was preoccupied with starting a construction business and was always working. Which meant Philip was left to fend for himself.

Feeling abandoned by his father, Philip got involved with drugs, got arrested and sentenced to two years in Frankfurt's Maasberg Juvenile Detention Center. Maasberg was an adult prison, that was converted into a detention center for juveniles. But given the fact that it was designed to house murderers and other dangerous criminals, there was nothing juvenile about it.

When Philip got to Maasberg and saw the kind of life he would have if he continued using drugs and getting in trouble, he decided that wasn't what he wanted. And instead of associating with gangs and troublemakers, Philip used his time in detention to improve himself. He earned his GED, developed his communication skills and learned to use his personality to manipulate others for his advantage.

At the end of his sentence, Philip went back to live with his father, and when Pero saw how mature Philip had become in detention, he put him to work in his construction business. To ensure Philip learned the business from the bottom up, Pero started him as a laborer on a construction site, where Philip relied on his communication skills to influence the other workers and improve their productivity.

When his father saw how well Philip got along with all the employees, he promoted him and made him a supervisor. Over the next few years, Philip got married, bought a house and tried to start a family. Unable to conceive, the couple blamed one another for their infertility, and a year later, they divorced. Depressed, Philip began drinking and not showing up for work.

"I understand you're having problems," Pero said. "But your behavior reflects negatively on me, and I can't have it."

"That's right, I forgot. All you care about is how what I'm going through affects you. It's always been that way. Well, it won't affect you anymore because I quit."

After he quit his job, Philip started spending time at a local Frankfurt casino and decided gambling would be the way he would support himself. He withdrew his savings from the bank, started to gamble and lost it all in less than a couple of weeks. Determined to win his money back, Philip started asking people at the construction company for loans. When Pero found out Philip was soliciting his employees for money, he called Ljubica and asked for her help.

"Can you please reach out to Philip?" Pero asked. "I'm afraid he's becoming addicted to gambling, and I can't get through to him."

Distraught by what she heard, Ljubica tried calling Philip, but he wouldn't return her calls, so she sent him a letter. In the letter, she told Philip how much she loved him, and wanted to offer her support, and to please call her.

Along with the letter, Ljubica enclosed a check for a thousand dollars to help Philip get by while he looked for another job. But instead of using the money to support himself, Philip went back to the casino and gambled it away. Broke again and desperate, Philip had no choice but to call his mother.

"I got your letter, Mother, and I want to thank you for the money. I needed it," Philip said.

"I'm glad you called, Son. Your father told me you quit your job and are spending your time at a casino gambling."

"No, not anymore. I've stopped," Philip replied.

"I'm glad to hear that. Have you looked for another job?"

"I have, but I think instead of working for someone, I want to go into business for myself."

"What kind of business?"

"I want to open a Croatian restaurant. Since there isn't anything like it in Frankfurt, I know it would do very well."

"Do you know how to run a restaurant?" Ljubica questioned.

"Once I secure a location, I plan on coming to Osijek and have you help me. You're the smartest business person I know."

"Have you started looking for locations?"

"I have, but they all want a deposit to secure the lease."

"How much?"

"Most of them want twenty-five thousand dollars."

Recognizing the money was her chance to get close to her son again, Ljubica agreed. "I'll wire you the money tomorrow morning."

"Are you kidding? Thank you, Mother. And as I said, as soon as I secure a location, I'll come to Osijek."

Ljubica sent Philip the money, and instead of using it to secure a location, he returned to the casino, lost it, and called his mother again.

"How's the hunt for a location going?" Ljubica asked.

"I found the perfect place in a great section of Frankfurt, but the owner wants more than twenty-five thousand you gave me to secure it."

"How much more?"

"Another twenty-five thousand."

"Fifty-thousand dollars? That's a lot of deposit money. Are you sure these people aren't taking advantage of you?"

"You're right, Mother," Philip said. "As perfect as this location is, and as much as I want to do it, I'll tell them the deposit is too much and walk away from the deal as you suggest."

Satisfied Philip was listening to her, Ljubica felt the deal must be legitimate and agreed to give him the additional money. "I'll wire you another twenty-five thousand today."

"Thank you so much, Mother. I'll pay you back. I love you."

"I love you, too, Son," Ljubica said, grateful to be getting close to her son again.

As he did with the original twenty-five thousand, Philip took the additional money and gambled it away again. But before he could call his mother again, she called him.

"Philip, I've got some terrible news."

"What is it, Mother?"

"Blanka and Nikola were killed in a car accident in France."

Not having seen his sister since they were kids and still harboring resentment, Philip didn't care she was dead. But he knew he'd have to sound distraught to get the additional money he wanted from Ljubica.

"Oh my God, that's terrible. Are you okay, Mother?"

"No. I'm still in shock, and so is Dario."

"I'm so sorry to hear that."

"I'm having their bodies brought back to Osijek for burial, and I want you to be here for the funerals."

"When are they?" Philip asked.

"Next Thursday. I'll send you a plane ticket and put you up at the Royal. And after the funerals, you can stay in Osijek and work with me."

"That sounds good, Mother. And again, I'm so sorry." Philip arrived in Osijek on the day of the funerals and discovered Dario was living with his mother.

And even though Philip and Dario had never met, since Dario was part Serbian and not full-blooded Croatian, Philip disliked him.

Dario experienced Pero's hatred for Serbians when he was thirteen, and he and Blanka went to Pero's fiftieth birthday party. Knowing his grandfather loved the accordion, Dario learned to play a special birthday song to surprise him. Impressed, Pero let Dario use his rare Croatian accordion for the song. When Dario started to play, and his grandfather recognized the song as Serbian, he became irate, grabbed the accordion out of Dario's hands, and slapped him across the face.

"You can't play that Serbian shit in this Croatian house," he said as he took the accordian and walked out of the room. Seeing how hateful his grandfather was toward his Serbian heritage, Dario never saw him again.

Both funerals for Dario's parents were held at Harpers Funeral Home, the oldest funeral home in Osijek, and the place that handled all the Kvaternik family funerals. When Dario and his grandmother got to Harpers for the memorial the night before the funerals, his grandfather Stanko and at least a hundred Croatian, Serbian, and Jewish friends of his parents were waiting to pay their respects. And when Dario saw his parents in their coffins, he broke down.

"I miss you both so much," Dario said through his tears.

Blanka was different than her brother. She was thoughtful, considerate and respectful. She was also ambitious, putting herself through culinary school working at the Royal with her mother. When Philip saw the wonderful life his sister had growing up in Osijek with Ljubica and compared it to the troubled life he had growing up in Germany with Pero, he hated his sister and mother even more.

After the funerals, Ljubica invited the mourners back to the Hotel Royal for refreshments. But instead of supporting his mother and Dario in their time of sorrow, Philip got drunk and became belligerent.

"You're not full-blooded Croatian; you're a mutt," Philip said to Dario.

"And you are full-blooded," Dario replied. "Full-blooded asshole."

"Stop it," Ljubica yelled as she stood in between the two men.

"I'm disappointed in you, Philip," she said.

"What do you mean, Mother?"

"Your contemptuous attitude toward the death of your sister and your lack of empathy for me having lost a daughter and Dario having lost both his parents is unbelievable. You don't love me; all I am to you is money."

"That's not true, Mother. I do love you."

"Enough. From now on, you'll have to come up with the money you need on your own."

"But you can't do that. I'm your son. You can't abandon me again. What about my business opportunity?"

The Picture Box

"There's no business opportunity; you lied to me to get the money you needed to gamble. I love you, Philip, but I can't help you anymore. I'm sorry."

Angry that his mother refused to give him more money, Philip went back to Frankfurt to the casino and asked to use his high-roller status to borrow money to gamble. Telling them that his father would guarantee the loan. Aware of Pero's impeccable business reputation, the casino agreed and over the next month, Philip borrowed and lost a hundred thousand dollars.

When casino management finally called in Philip's markers, and he couldn't pay, they called his father for the money. Unaware of Philip's agreement with the casino, Pero refused to pay the debt, and the casino threatened to have Philip arrested. Not able to get help from his mother, Philip asked a waitress he was dating if she knew anybody that could help him.

"I do," she said, "his name is Karl Schmidt, and he loans people money for a living."

"How do you know him?"

"That's not important. Do you want to meet him?"

Having run out of options, Philip agreed, "Yes."

The woman set up a meeting in one of the casino bars and told Philip that Schmidt would be sitting by himself at a table having a drink. As Philip walked into the bar, he saw a man he assumed was Schmidt, sitting alone at a table smoking a cigarette. Schmidt was a six-foot-five, well-built, forty-year-old man with long black hair and dressed in an expensive silk suit.

"Karl Schmidt?" Philip asked as he walked over to the table.

"That's right," Schmidt replied, lighting another cigarette.

"I'm Philip Truntic, the man you're supposed to meet."

"Sit down. Would you like a drink?" Schmidt asked.

"No, thank you," Philip replied as he sat down.

"My friend says you owe the casino a hundred thousand dollars?" Schmidt said.

"That's right," Philip replied.

"That's a lot of money. What happened?"

"I have a gambling problem, and it got out of control."

"I should say. Did my friend tell you anything about me?"

"Just that you loan people money."

"I don't loan money," Schmidt replied. "I work for people that do."

"You mean the Mafia?"

"We prefer the name syndicate. Do you have collateral to back up the loan?"

"I have a house, but I've already leveraged it, so it's not worth anything."

"And that's the only thing of value you have?"

"Yes."

"What about your family? Do they have anything?"

"My mother has money and a house in Osijek, Croatia."

"Then why don't you ask her to pay your debt?"

"I can't. We're not close."

"That's too bad, cause without collateral, we can't do business," Schmidt said as he started to get up from the table.

"Wait. I know where I can get the collateral. A member of my mother's family was a general in the Croatian army working with the Nazis during World War Two, and he gave my mother some of the gold the Germans left in Croatia after the war, and according to my father, her ex-husband, she has it hidden in her house in Osijek."

"I've heard about the Nazi's leaving gold in Croatia," Schmidt said.

"That's right. And like I said, my mother has some of it, and all I have to do is go there and find it."

"You know there's interest on the money I loan you," Schmidt said, lighting another cigarette.

"How much?"

"Twenty-five thousand dollars."

"Twenty-five percent, that's a lot," Philip replied.

"If you can find the money from someone else for less, you should do it."

"Okay, I'll pay it," Philip replied.

"Then my associates will take a chance and loan you the money," Schmidt said.

"Thank you."

"But if there's no gold and you aren't able to pay back the loan, I'll be forced to make something terminal happen to you and your whole family. Is that understood?"

"Yes," Philip replied.

"And one more thing, I'll be going with you to Osijek to protect my investment."

"Who will I say you are when we get to Osijek?" Philip asked.

"You'll tell them we're partners in the real estate business in Germany and want to expand into Croatia. And since you know Osijek, we're there to find real estate investments."

"Fine."

"Now, while I take care of your debt with the casino, you make arrangements for us to leave for Osijek first thing tomorrow morning, and I'll meet you at the Frankfurt airport. Now, how about that drink?"

"Yeah. Now I need it," Philip replied.

CHAPTER II

In Vegas, Dario performed six nights a week from nine until two the following morning, so by the end of the week, he was exhausted and looked forward to getting some rest. This particular morning, when he got back to his apartment, got in bed, and started to fall asleep, his cell phone rang. Dario wanted to ignore the call but saw it was from his best friend, Paul Novak, in Osijek. Dario and Paul had been best friends since they were kids and frequently talked. But never at three-thirty in the morning so Dario knew the call must be important.

"Hello. Paul, is everything okay?"

"No, Dario, your grandmother had a heart attack this morning."

"Is she okay?"

"She died, Dario."

"I just spoke to her at the end of last week, and she sounded fine," Dario said in disbelief.

"I'm so sorry, Dario, it was sudden."

"Was she at home when it happened?"

"No, she was in the Dom Sunce assisted living facility."

"What? Why was she in assisted living?"

"There was a fire at her house, and since you weren't here, your uncle Philip moved her into Dom Sunce to be taken care of."

"Fire? When?"

"Listen, Dario, it's better if I tell you about it when I see you. Are you able to come back for her memorial and funeral?"

"When are they?"

"Her memorial is next Thursday night, and her funeral is on Friday morning."

"I'll be there. Listen, Paul, thank you for calling me, but I can't talk anymore. I'll call you with my flight information as soon as I have it."

"I understand. And again, I'm so sorry," Paul said and ended the call.

"My sweet grandmother," Dario said as he collapsed on the bed crying. "I'm so sorry I wasn't there to look after you."

Two days later, Dario left for Osijek, and on the twelve-hour flight, he couldn't stop thinking about his grandmother and the special times they shared. Like the summer weekend trips to her cabin on the Adriatic Sea, where Dario and his parents would swim while his grandmother prepared her favorite Croatian dishes. And the parties she would throw at her house and the Hotel Royal and would have Dario sing. He remembered how she comforted him when his parents got killed and how she helped him get his visa and gave him money to move to America. And as Dario thought more about her, he was overcome with regret that he hadn't seen her before she died.

The Picture Box

When Dario landed at the Osijek International Airport, located twenty miles southeast of the city, Paul was waiting for him outside the baggage claim. Paul was five years older than Dario and ruggedly handsome. Dario and Paul shared a love of music, and in high school, they formed a band and performed throughout the city. Dario sang, and Paul accompanied him on the guitar and sang backup. While Dario was popular with all the younger girls in Osijek, Paul dated the older girls and would share his sexual escapades with Dario, who jealously looked forward to hearing them. Ljubica liked Paul and felt he was a good influence on Dario, so she paid for an apartment to give them their independence.

While Dario and Paul had always planned to go to America together and sing, when Paul's father passed away and his mother needed his help, Paul had to give up his dream and stay in Osijek. After Dario left, Paul became a fireman and promised Dario he would look after his grandmother while he was away. And until she died, he did, and Dario was grateful.

After Dario picked up his luggage, Paul drove him to Osijek.

I'm sorry again about grandma," Paul said.

"Thank you. Is Harpers handling her funeral?"

"Yes, and she's being buried at St. Anas Cemetery. Your uncle made all the arrangements. He's also having a memorial for her tonight, and her funeral is tomorrow morning. I made a hotel reservation for you at the Royal."

Dario knew his grandmother wanted her funeral handled by Harpers, and to be buried at St. Anas, next to her second husband Hrusto, and near Blanka. Hrusto was a well-known Croatian jeweler who his grandmother married a few years after Dario left for America, so he never got to know him.

"Tell me more about the fire at her house," Dario said.

"It happened when your grandmother wasn't home.

It looks like she left an iron on, and accidentally set the house on fire."

"Why didn't you tell me about it when it happened?"

"It's still under investigation, and I was instructed not to say anything to anybody."

"By who?"

"Tomo Babic."

"What does Tomo have to do with it?"

"He's the Chief of Police in Osijek now."

"Tomo Babic, the class asshole is Chief of Police?"

"Yeah, after you left, Tomo became a policeman and then Captain. And then last year, he and Sanja got married."

"They did?" Dario asked.

Dario and Sanja were boyfriend and girlfriend in school and had always planned on being married. But Tomo also loved Sanja and tried everything to get her and Dario to break up. Dario remembered Tomo as a bully, who not only made fun of Dario's singing, but openly hated Dario for leaving the country and not fighting for Croatia in the War of Independence.

"You're not going to America to sing," Tomo said to Dario before he left. "You're going because you're a coward and have no allegiance to Croatia or Osijek."

Since Dario survived the war, while so many others didn't, he often thought about what Tomo said and wondered if he was right.

"And you said my uncle put her in assisted living after the fire?"

"Yes. He felt she'd be better off there than living by herself."

"She'd be better off? He meant he'd be better off. Was everything in the house destroyed?"

"Just about."

"What about the family photos my grandmother had hung on the walls in the living room?"

"Three of them survived the fire and were given to the woman who owns the assisted living facility."

"Why did she get them?"

"The law in Croatia says that if a person dies alone in an assisted living facility, the owner of the facility has the legal right to take their possessions and sell them to offset what they owe for their care."

"That's the law in Croatia?"

"Yes."

"I can't believe it. Who's the owner?"

"Her name is Vera Juric. She's a friend of your uncle's."

"A friend of my uncle's? That's interesting. Besides the owner of the assisted living facility, have you seen my uncle with anyone else?"

"Yeah, with some guy I didn't know."

"You don't recognize him?

"No. He's a big, mean-looking guy who showed up with your uncle a couple of days before the fire."

"And Tomo's handling the fire investigation?"

"Yeah."

"Then, I'll need to see him. What time is my grandmother's funeral tomorrow?"

"Saint Anas has it scheduled for ten in the morning."

Founded in 1748, Saint Anas is a famous graveyard in Croatia, established to accommodate the thousands of Croatians who died during the 1738 bubonic plague, World War Two, and War of Independence.

As they drove to the city, Dario was surprised to see the countryside of Osijek showed no signs of damage from the war. And despite the unpopulated areas left by the migration out of Croatia by the Serbs, Jews, and Gypsies before the war, new residential developments and business centers showed a renewed Osijek vibrancy.

When they pulled up in front of the Hotel Royal, Dario was pleased to see the famous hotel, despite having some façade damage from the war, had retained its original grandeur. Built in 1885 and located in the city center near the Korzo, the town square, the Royal is a prominent Croatian landmark near the famous Catholic Cathedral where Dario and his family attended mass. As Dario paused and looked at the hotel before he got out of the car, he remembered the wonderful times he shared there with his grandmother, having lunch and singing in the hotel restaurant.

"Does the hotel look like you remembered?"

"Yeah. A little scuffed up, but otherwise just the same."

"The memorial's tonight at seven-thirty. So, I'll pick you up at seven," Paul said as Dario got out of the car.

"See you then. And, Paul, I know we've talked about this before, about you having to stay in Osijek and not coming with me to America to sing, but I want to tell you again how grateful I am that you looked after my grandmother while I was gone."

"It was my pleasure. And besides, that's what best friends are for."

"And I'm also grateful you and Emily weren't hurt in the war."

"We weren't, but a lot of our friends were."

"I know, and I'm sorry."

"Me, too. I'll see you later."

As Paul drove away, Dario watched him go, then walked into the hotel to the second-floor registration desk where a white-haired seventy-five-year-old man, standing at the desk, greeted him.

"Welcome back to the Royal, Dario."

"I'm sorry, have we met before?" Dario replied.

"We have. I was your engineering teacher when you were in school."

"Mr. Horvat?"

"That's right. I understand why you didn't recognize me. I'm quite a bit older than I was then, and my lack of hair proves it."

"We're all quite a bit older. It's good to see you," Dario said as he shook his hand.

Before becoming a teacher, Horvat was a Nazi sympathizer during World War Two and openly backed Croatia's association with the Germans. When it became clear the Nazis were going to lose the war, Horvat broke away from the movement and became a teacher.

"Are you working here?" Dario asked.

"Yes. When the War of Independence started, the Croatian government cut the education budget and laid off teachers to support the army. That's when your grandmother hired me to manage the hotel for her, and I've been here ever since. I want to offer my condolences. Your grandmother was an incredible lady."

"Yes, she was."

"And you came back for her funeral?"

"Yes."

"Since I haven't seen you around, I thought you were killed in the war, like so many of my students."

"No. I went to America just as it was starting."

"That's right, now I remember. Your grandmother told me you went there to be a singer. Did things work out?"

"They did. I'm performing in a show in Las Vegas."

"Las Vegas. I've always wanted to go there."

"And you say there were a lot of your past students killed?"

"Unfortunately."

"But things are peaceful now, right?"

"Thank God."

"How's the Royal doing?"

"Ater the war, tourism picked up in Osijek, and we're doing okay."

"That's good. Who owns the hotel now?"

"The Croatian government."

"Well, I better get checked in and get ready for my grandmother's memorial," Dario said.

"At Harpers, I know."

"Will you be there?

"Yes, I want to pay my respects. How long will you be staying in Osijek?"

"A week."

"I put you in room 315. It was your grandmother's favorite."

"I remember. That's the room with the large balcony overlooking the Korzo."

"Your grandmother loved to spend time on that balcony and look out over the city. Can I have your passport, please?"

"Of course." Dario handed Horvat his passport. "Do you want a credit card for the room?"

"There's no charge for the room in remembrance of your grandmother."

"Thank you."

Horvat handed Dario a room key. "It's nice to have you back."

"It's nice to be back."

Dario took his luggage up to the room, unpacked it and walked out on the balcony. As Dario looked over the bustling Korzo, he heard the familiar sounds of both the tram bells from the iconic Qsijek electric tram and the tower bells from the nearby Cathedral of Saint Paul and Peter.

"I know you're here with me, Grandma, looking over the city we both love so much. God bless you."

Dario left the hotel, walked into the Korzo, and was pleased to see the places he frequented twenty years before were still there. Places like Vinoteka Vinta. The wine bar where he and Paul would go on Friday nights to drink excellent Croatian wines and sing. Dario and Paul were famous in the town and always drew a crowd and sometimes the police when the audience got drunk and rowdy.

He looked through a window at the inside of the empty bar expecting to see the old-world décor he remembered: the dark colors, dim lighting, and uncomfortable wooden stools. But instead saw a modern lounge with vibrant colors, contemporary lighting, and oversized leather couches. The small stage that was just big enough for him and Paul, with two microphones, an antiquated sound system, and old track lighting, was now a large performance stage with updated lighting and several mics.

At that moment, the bar's front door opened, and Drazen Maric, the sixty-five-year-old owner, walked out. Drazen was a small, fat man with thick black hair and beard.

"Dario, is that you?"

"Yes, Drazen."

"It's so good to see you?" Drazen replied.

"It's good to see you, too," Dario said, as he hugged Drazen. "You still own the place?"

"Of course. What else would I do?"

"You updated it. It looks great."

"It got damaged in the war, so I didn't have a choice. I heard about your grandmother. I'm so sorry."

"Thank you."

"You here for her funeral?"

"Yes."

"Where are you living now?"

"In America. Las Vegas."

"Are you singing?"

"Yes. I have a show in one of the casinos."

"Figures. I knew you'd be famous someday."

"How's business?" Dario asked.

"It's good. We get a steady crowd of locals and quite a few American tourists."

"Does Paul come in very often?"

"Every once in a while. When he does, we still talk about when you guys sang here."

"Yeah, that was fun."

"Listen, how long are you going to be in Osijek?"

"A week or so."

"Well, how about you and Paul coming back one night and singing? I know the crowd would love it. And so would I."

"I'll talk to Paul and let you know."

"Good. Well, I've got to get ready to open. I hope to see you and Paul. Goodbye."

"Goodbye."

Drazen went back inside the bar, and Dario continued down the Korzo to IPK, the famous Croatian pastry shop, where Dario and his school friends would meet for a delicious pastry before class. To this day, IPK is renowned for its pastry specialties, including Krempita Sa Slagom, a traditional Croatian cake and pudding delicacy. Dario walked into the shop and approached a woman behind a counter.

"Can I help you, sir?" she said.

"Do you still make Krempita Sa Slagom?"

"Of course, it's our specialty."

"I'd like a piece to go, please."

"Certainly."

The woman gave Dario the dessert and he walked out of the bakery and down the Korzo to another familiar place, Café Mignon. The restaurant where Dario and his grandmother would have lunch a few times a month. Besides a menu of excellent Croatian foods, the Café also has a long list of specialty Croatian coffees.

As he walked into the restaurant, he heard the familiar sounds of piano playing. He recognized the song as one of his grandmother's favorites and remembered her always asking him to sing it for her. So, in her memory, Dario started to sing and imagined his grandmother smiling with admiration. When he finished singing, the restaurant guests applauded, and Dario sat at a table.

"That was beautiful," a waitress said as she walked up.

"Thank you."

"Can I get you something to eat?"

"No, thank you. I'd just like a Kava S Mlijekom, please."

"Certainly."

Kava S Mlijekom, or coffee with warm milk, is a popular Croatian coffee, and Café Mignon makes the best in Osijek. After he got his coffee, Dario walked onto the restaurant's patio, sat down, and watched the crowds of people in the Korzo go in and out of the various shops. And again, he thought of his grandmother and the fun they had people watching.

After he finished his coffee and krempita, Dario left the café and walked down to the Red Star movie theatre. The Red

Star is where Dario and his friends saw all the latest features and have a bag of roasted chestnuts from the chestnut cart out front. And while the theatre was renovated after the War of Independence and changed its name to Kino Europa, the familiar fragrant smell of roasted chestnuts still draws Osijek's population like a magnet.

As he stood outside the theatre, Dario remembered all the fun Friday nights he and Paul had going to the movies. They would get dates and sit in the back of the theater, make out and see which one could get their dates blouses unbuttoned first. Paul always won, and it made Dario mad.

"What's your secret?" Dario asked him.

"It's all in the wrist," Paul replied as he laughed and made circles with his right wrist pretending to undo buttons.

But as happy as the memories of the Red Star made Dario, his best memory came as he passed Varnai, the photography shop near the church. Varnai was where Dario's parents took him as a baby to have his picture taken. Dario remembered the shop owner, a Jewish friend of his grandmother's, had a photo of Dario at age four standing next to Blanka, wearing a white jumpsuit and sitting on a rocking horse, blown up and hung it in the shop window as an advertisement. Dario never forgot that picture, and when he knew he was coming back to Osijek, he planned to find out if the shop owner still had the negative.

Before going back to the Royal to meet Paul, Dario went into the Cathedral to pray for his grandmother and parents. Built in the neo-Gothic style in 1898 by Bishop Joseph Strossmayer, the Cathedral is the tallest building in Croatia with four huge towers housing the bells Dario heard from his balcony at the Royal. The church seats three thousand and has multiple, large, ornate stained-glass windows surrounding an exquisitely painted ceiling reminiscent of the Vatican's Sistine Chapel.

As Dario walked into the church, he made the sign of the cross and knelt in one of the pews. As he looked around, he could see signs of damage caused by the War of Independence. From cracks in the walls and floors to the discolored paint on several of the interior columns. As he looked at a statue of Jesus on the altar nailed to the cross, Dario closed his eyes, said a silent prayer, then left.

Instead of walking back to the Royal, Dario got on the tram. The electric Tramvaj that Dario saw from his hotel balcony started operating in 1884 and symbolizes Osijek. The original horse-drawn version got replaced by the electric tram in 1926 and runs throughout the city. It picks up passengers starting at the Osijek train station and makes its last stop at the Cathedral.

When he got back to the Royal, Paul and his wife Emily were waiting for him outside. Dario introduced Paul and Emily when they were in high school and was the best man at their wedding. Emily had long black hair, piercing black eyes, a petite slender body, and a smile that lit up the world. And even though she was twenty years older, she looked like she did when they were in school.

"It's good to see you, Emily. You look great." Dario said as he hugged her.

"You look good, too," Emily replied.

"What about me?" Paul asked. "I look good, too, right?"

"No, not that good," Dario said, laughing.

"Smartass," Paul replied.

"It's good to have you back," Emily said. "I'm so sorry about grandma. I miss her."

"We all do," Paul replied. "We have to go, or we'll be late for the memorial."

As they drove to the funeral home, they reminisced about their days together in school.

"Paul told me Mr. Horvat works at the Royal," Emily said.

"That's right. Grandmother hired him to manage the place after he lost his teaching job."

"I was sorry he lost his job. He loved teaching," Emily said.

"I remember how much we fooled around in his class," Paul said.

"You two fooled around, I studied. And Dario spent his time flirting with Sanja," Emily said.

"Sanja and Tomo are coming to the wake," Paul said.

"I still can't believe Sanja married Tomo," Dario said.

"In school, she thought he was a jerk."

"Circumstances change. When you left, she needed to move on, and he was here," Emily replied. "And besides being married to Tomo, Sanja's also a nursing supervisor at Osijek Medical Center and works with children with cancer."

"I'm happy for her," Dario said.

"Really?" Paul asked. "You're not upset she married the jerk who hated your guts for leaving and not fighting in the war?"

"It's been twenty years. Think Tomo still feels that way?" Dario asked.

"He's still a jerk," Paul replied.

When they got to the funeral home, they saw hundreds of people standing outside waiting to go in to pay their respects to Ljubica.

"Who are all these people?" Dario asked.

"People your grandmother helped through the years," Paul replied as an older white-haired man dressed in a black suit walked up to Dario.

"Dario, my name is Stjepan Vranjes, and I'm the owner of the funeral home. I met you twenty years ago when I handled your parents' funeral. But you probably don't remember."

"I'm sorry, I don't. But it's nice meeting you again," Dario replied and shook his hand.

"Quite a turnout, isn't it?" Vranjes said.

"Unbelievable."

"Your grandmother was a very respected woman. Come on, and I'll take you in."

Vranjes escorted Dario, Paul and Emily into the main viewing room of the funeral home, where at least a hundred people were standing in front of an altar covered with flowers waiting to view Ljubica's coffin and pay their respects. Next to the coffin were several enlarged pictures of Ljubica taken with Blanka.

One of the pictures, taken when his mother was in her thirties and Ljubica was in her fifties, showed the two women laughing and blowing out candles on a birthday cake. They looked like sisters. Blanka had long black hair and captivating black eyes, while Ljubica had long flowing silver hair and piercing blue eyes. Seeing the loving way the women looked at one another and knowing they were both gone, Dario teared up.

"God bless you both."

Dario looked around the room and saw his uncle Philip standing next to an older, attractive, well-dressed blonde-haired woman. Now in his late fifties, Philip was thin with sunken cheeks, dark circles under his eyes, and deep age and stress lines on his face. He had thinning grey hair and a thin grey moustache and was wearing a black suit. When he saw Dario, he deliberately turned his back and said something to the woman.

Standing behind Philip, Dario saw Sanja and Tomo, dressed in his police uniform. Sanja had long blonde hair, hypnotic brown eyes, and a small beauty mark on her right cheek and was just as beautiful as she was when she was seventeen. Tomo also looked like he did in school. He had close-cropped black hair and a black beard and moustache. And when he and Dario saw one another, Tomo didn't smile and gave Dario a threatening look.

Standing near Sanja and Tomo was Mr. Horvat with another older man Dario didn't recognize, and next to them was Father Josip. Father Josip was a distinguished-looking gray-haired, eighty-five-year-old priest who was a good friend of Dario's grandmother. Through the years, Ljubica had donated large sums of money to the church, and Josip always praised her generosity. When the priest saw Dario, he smiled and walked over.

"Dario, it's good to see you. I'm so sorry about your grandmother, but she's at peace with God now."

"Thank you, Father. It's quite a turnout."

"She was loved."

"Will you be delivering the funeral sermon tomorrow at her gravesite?" Dario asked.

"Yes," Josip said. "And I hope you'll say a few words."

"Absolutely."

"Well then, I'll see you tomorrow morning. Goodnight."

"Goodnight."

As Father Josip left the funeral home, Philip and the woman he was with walked up.

"So, you finally came back to Osijek. And all it took was my mother's death," Philip said.

"I'm surprised you remembered she was your mother," Dario replied. "The only time you knew her was when you needed money."

"Is that right? You were the one that took her money and ran away to America."

"And you left her here alone to die."

"You're still a half-Croatian mutt; you know that?" Philip said.

"And you're still a whole Croatian asshole."

"Dario, my name is Vera Juric," the woman said to Dario, "the owner of the assisted living facility where your grandmother was. I want to offer my condolences."

"You mean the facility where she died?"

"That's right," Philip replied. "She had heart problems and needed care."

"She did, Dario," Vera said.

"She never told me anything about problems with her heart, and I talked to her all the time."

"You're welcome to come to the facility and see the kind of care we provided your grandmother," Vera said.

"I'll do that."

"Come on, Vera, let's go. He's not worth the explanation," Philip said as he took Vera's arm and walked away as Sanja walked up.

"It's good to see you again, Dario. Sorry about grandma."

"Thank you. Emily tells me that you and Tomo got married and that you're a supervising nurse at Osijek Medical Center."

"Yes," Sanja replied.

"Congratulations."

"Thank you. And the last time I saw grandma, she told me your singing career in America was going well."

"Yeah, I'm performing in Las Vegas."

"That's great; it's what you always wanted. I went to the assisted living facility a few times to visit Grandma before she died," Sanja said.

"You did? Did she ever tell you she was having heart problems?"

"No, but heart attacks in older people can happen without warning. Your grandmother was eighty-five."

"I just wish I could have seen her again before she died."

"I know. I'm so sorry. On my last visit, Ljubica gave me a package to give to you."

"She did? That's strange. Did she think we'd see each other again?"

"I guess so."

"Did she tell you what it is?"

"No, she had it sealed and only wanted you to see it. I'll be working at the hospital tomorrow afternoon, so if you come by, I'll give it to you."

"Give him what?" Tomo asked as he walked up and put his arm around Sanja.

"Just something his grandmother gave me she wanted Dario to have."

"I understand you're handling the investigation of the fire at my grandmother's house?" Dario asked.

"That's right," Tomo replied. "We think an iron your grandmother left on caused it, but we're still investigating."

"Will you let me know what you find out?" Dario asked.

"If I have something to tell you," Tomo replied. "Sanja, we need to go. I have to work."

"Sorry again about grandma, Dario," Sanja said.

"Thank you."

As Tomo and Sanja left the funeral home, Paul, Emily, Mr. Horvat, and the man with him walked over.

"Dario, I have to get back to the hotel, but I wanted you to meet Mr. Meric, a good friend of your grandmother's and the owner of Varnai, the photography studio."

Meric was an old, bald, little Jewish man wearing thick bifocals. "It's nice seeing you again, Dario. Your grandmother talked about you often. She was proud of you."

"And I was proud of her. You said we've met before?"

"Yes. When you were a baby and your parents had me take your picture."

"I remember. That was the picture you hung up in your shop window?"

"That's right."

"I went to your shop earlier today to find out if you still have the negative. I'd like to have it."

"I do," Meric replied. "Come to the shop before you leave, and I'll give it to you. I also have a box of pictures your grandmother had me develop that she never picked up. I'll give you those, too."

"Thank you. I'll be there."

"Well, I'll see you back at the hotel, Dario," Horvat said.

"Thank you both for coming."

Horvat and Meric walked out, and Paul and Emily walked over.

"Are you ready to go?" Paul asked Dario.

"Yeah. Just let me say one last goodbye to my grandmother."

Dario walked up to his grandmother's casket.

"I love you, Grandmother, and I'm sorry I didn't keep my promise and come back to Osijek to see you," he said, and kissed her cheek. "Rest in peace."

CHAPTER III

The next morning Dario, carrying flowers for his grandmother's grave, took the tram to St. Anas before her funeral to visit his parents' gravesites and walk through the cemetery. St. Anas is known as the Gallery of Sculptures because of the hundreds of sculptures done by famous Croatian artists that populate the fifty-four acre, ten-thousand grave cemetery.

As Dario walked through the graveyard, he recognized the names of several of his college friends killed in the war.

"I can't believe it. Why did it have to happen?"

After saying a prayer at his parent's graves, he went back to his grandmother's gravesite. Paul, Emily, Philip, and Vera, all holding flowers, and Father Josip, carrying a bible, were standing next to Ljubica's coffin. As Dario walked up, Father Josip approached the casket and opened his bible.

"We are here today to celebrate the life of Ljubica Kvaternik," Father Josip said. "She was a devoted mother and grandmother and always helped those in need in Osijek. And while she's gone from our lives, she will live on forever in our hearts. And her soul will be eternally in the comfort of the Lord. Amen. Dario and Philip, would either of you like to say a few words?"

"Yes," Dario said as he moved close to the casket and placed flowers on the lid.

"Grandmother, I will always remember the love and support you showed my mother and me, and never forget the woman you were and the time we spent together. I wish we could have spent more. God bless you."

Dario stepped back, and Josip turned to Philip. "Philip, would you like to say a few words?"

Philip moved close to the casket. "Rest in peace, mother," he said and put his flowers on the coffin, then stepped back, and Josip approached the casket again.

"May the Lord bless you and watch over you, Ljubica," Josip said. "And may his light shine upon you and bring you peace. In the name of the Father, the Son, and the Holy Ghost. Amen."

"Thank you, Father. That was lovely," Dario said.

"You're welcome, Dario. Will I see you again before you leave?"

"I'm planning on coming to mass on Sunday."

"Good. And bring Paul and Emily with you."

As Josip walked away with Philip, Vera approached Dario.

"Are you still coming to see the facility?"

"I was planning on coming later this afternoon, if that works?"

"I'll be there."

Vera walked away and Dario, Paul and Emily stayed at the gravesite and watched as Ljubica's coffin was lowered into the grave. "I love you, Grandmother, and don't worry, I'll sing for you again."

They left the graveyard and Paul and Emily took Dario back to the Royal.

"Thank you for inviting us today, Dario," Emily said as she hugged him.

"Yeah. Thank you," Paul said. "How about joining us for lunch?"

"Can't. I've got to see Sanja at the hospital; she's got something for me from my grandmother."

"You need a ride?" Paul asked.

"No thanks, I'll take the tram. I'll catch up with you later."

"Yes, you will. We're having our twentieth-class reunion tonight at Hotel Osijek. It got remodeled after the war, and it's beautiful. A lot of our old classmates will be there to do some singing, dancing, and drinking."

"The Hotel Osijek? Isn't that where we had our college graduation party," Dario asked.

"That's right. That was the night you got drunk, and the hotel had to call the police," Paul said, smiling.

"You both got drunk," Emily said.

"What time's the party?" Dario asked.

"Eight," Paul replied.

"I'll be there," Dario said. "And thanks again for coming today."

After Emily and Paul left, Dario took the tram to Osijek Medical Center the largest hospital in Croatia, and found Sanja in the Children's Cancer Ward looking after a young boy having chemotherapy. Dario always thought her decision to become a nurse and care for the sick was perfect. Besides being beautiful, Sanja was also intelligent, humble, loving, and caring, all the traits a nurse needs. And when it came to their relationship, she always made Dario feel important and loved no matter how immature and self-absorbed he acted. After Sanja finished her shift, she met Dario for coffee in the hospital cafeteria.

"It's nice to have you back. It's been a long time," Sanja said.

"Too long," Dario replied. "And the work you're doing with the kids is incredible."

"Thank you. But it's the kids that are incredible. Many of them are fighting a terminal disease and refuse to give up. They have remarkable courage. We can all learn a lesson from them."

"Yeah."

"I wanted to tell you again, how sorry I am about your grandmother. She was a very special lady."

"She felt the same way about you. How have you been?"

"Good. I'm doing what I love, and the rest of my life is going well, too, now. After you stayed in America, it took me a while to move on, but then Tomo and I got together, and things got better. And you? Besides singing, are you seeing anyone?"

"I've had a few relationships, but nothing serious. You're hard to replace," Dario said, smiling.

Sanja didn't respond, and reached into her backpack, took out a small, sealed package, and handed it to Dario.

"It's heavy. I wonder what it is."

At that moment, Sanja got a text and looked at her phone.

"I have to go. Tomo's outside."

"Thank you for giving me this. Can I see you again before I go back to America?"

"I don't think that's a good idea."

"I understand," Dario said as they exchanged a hug.

"Be well," Sanja said, then walked away.

Dario wanted to stop her and tell her he still loved her but decided against it. She was settled and happy, and he didn't want to cause any problems.

On the tram ride back to the Royal, Dario opened the package and found a ring and a display box containing a two-pound gold bar. The ring was a simple gold wedding ring with the German inscription 'Der wahre Schatz Kommt. Nach, dem wir gestorben sind'engraved on the inside of the band. And since Dario had forgotten most of the German he learned as a boy in Croatia, he couldn't translate the phrase. He looked closer at the gold bar, and on one side was the design of an eagle atop a Swastika, and on the other side was a skull and cross bones and the word 'Todesschwadron', meaning death squad, and the date 1942. Realizing the date was during World War Two, Dario wondered how his grandmother got it and why she gave it to him.

When Dario got back to the Royal, Horvat was at the reception desk.

"How was your grandmother's funeral?"

"It was good. Father Josip did a great job."

"He's known your grandmother since they were kids and was a good friend."

"Yes, he was. Can you do me a favor?" Dario asked.

"If I can."

"Since there isn't a safe in my room, can you hold something in the hotel safe for me?"

"Absolutely."

Dario handed Horvat the package containing the ring and gold bar. "Looks important," Horvat said.

"It is. It's from my grandmother."

Dario watched as Horvat opened the safe under the reception desk and set the package inside.

"Thank you. I'm going to a class reunion at Hotel Osijek, so I'll pick it up tonight when I get back."

"No problem. Have a good time and tell everyone I said hi."

"I will."

The Hotel Osijek is within walking distance from the Royal near the Cathedral. It was built in 1977 and updated and made larger in 2004 after the war. Now a four-star hotel with sixteen floors, 147 rooms, and a huge banquet room, the hotel is used by Osijek's population for special occasions like weddings and graduations.

As Dario walked into the hotel, he remembered his college graduation party. That night, before going to the hotel, Dario, Sanja, Paul, and Emily, dressed in graduation gowns and tuxedos, went to his grandmother's house to have their pictures taken holding their diplomas.

"I'm so proud of you all," Ljubica said as she took the pictures.

"Thank you, Grandma," they all said.

"Now go to your graduation party and have fun. You deserve it. But be careful."

"Don't worry, Grandma," Paul said. "I'll take care of him."

"But who's going to take of you?" Ljubica said to Paul.

"I'll take care of them both," Sanja said.

"Now that I believe," Ljubica said, smiling.

That night, contrary to what Sanja promised, Dario and Paul got drunk, and the police got called; in other words, everyone had a good time. But now, as Dario walked to the hotel, he wondered how many of his classmates were still alive and would be at the celebration.

When Dario walked into the hotel lobby, he was surprised at how beautiful it was. Besides modern furniture and exquisite Croatian artwork, glass elevators allowed a lobby view as they ascended. Dario stepped into one of the elevators and enjoyed the view as he rode to the hotel's top floor.

As he walked off the elevator, he heard a band playing and people partying in one of the banquet rooms. He walked into the room and saw at least a hundred people, including Paul and Emily, dancing to a live rock and roll band. And despite everybody being twenty years older, to Dario they looked like they did at their college graduation party. When Paul and Emily saw Dario, they stopped dancing and came over.

"Did you see Sanja?" Emily asked.

"Yes, and she's doing remarkable work at the hospital."

"Did she give you what your grandmother wanted you to have?" Paul asked.

"Yes, but I'll tell you about it later; I want to party. Come on, Emily, dance with me. You don't mind, do you?" he asked Paul.

"Mind? It'll give me a rest."

The Picture Box

"You mean it will give the tops of my feet a rest," Emily said.

As Dario and Emily danced, several people recognized Dario and came over to say hello, and after the song finished, Paul walked onto the bandstand and grabbed a microphone.

"Can I have your attention, please? I want to take this opportunity to welcome you all to our twenty-year class reunion." Everybody clapped. "But before we go back to partying, I want to take a moment and acknowledge the classmates missing from our celebration. Can we have the lights lowered, please?"

The lights dimmed, and a large video screen dropped from the ceiling behind the bandstand and showed the names and photos of various young men and women killed in the War of Independence. After the photos finished, everyone clapped again.

"I know we all miss them and send them our prayers."

Then the lights came up, and the screen got raised.

"Now, I want to ask my best friend Dario Dimitric to come up to the stage. You may not know this, but Dario is headlining a show in Las Vegas. Lucky bastard."

As Dario walked onto the bandstand and took the microphone, only a few people clapped, and before he spoke, he looked over the crowd.

"I know I wasn't here to fight for Croatia's independence, but after my parents died I got an opportunity to go to America and pursue a dream that you all know I've had since I was a boy. A dream my grandmother, before she died, helped me to achieve. And while I wasn't here with you physically, I never stopped thinking about all my friends here and praying for your safety. And I never stopped loving Croatia and especially Osijek, and I feel blessed to be back."

The crowd stayed silent for a moment, then spurred on by Paul, everyone clapped and cheered.

"Okay, now for a real treat," Paul said. "Dario is going to sing a song for us."

Everyone clapped as Dario stepped up to the mic.

"After I found out my grandmother died, and knew I was coming back to Osijek for her funeral, I took the opportunity to write an original song to celebrate the city she and I both love so much."

Everyone clapped again as Dario gave the band a cue, and they started to play.

"The title of the song is Spava li moj Osijek grad kao nekada? Does my city of Osijek sleep as before?" Then he sang the song about how peaceful Osijek was before the War of Independence and how he hoped the city had been resting peacefully since the war.

After Dario finished the song, everyone cheered, and Paul moved next to him.

"Wasn't that beautiful? Not as good as I would have done, but what do you expect? He's still learning." The crowd laughed. "Now, let's get back to the party."

Later that night, Dario said goodnight to Paul and Emily. "I need to go back to the Royal and get some sleep. Will I see you guys tomorrow morning at church? Don't forget, I told Father Josip you'd be there."

"Ah, I'm not sure we'll be able to make it," Paul said.

"We'll be there," Emily said.

"That's what I meant," Paul replied.

"Great. See you then. Goodnight."

Dario walked out of the hotel and saw Sanja sitting at a cab stand.

"Hello. What are you doing here?"

"Waiting for a cab. I had to work a double shift at the hospital and came down to the Korzo to get a drink."

"Where's Tomo?"

"He's at a police training seminar until tomorrow. How was the reunion?"

"It was great. You were missed."

"Was the entire class there?"

"Everyone able."

"Sad, isn't it?"

"Very. Listen, I'd like to get a cup of coffee before I go back to the Royal. Would you care to join me? As a friend."

"Okay, as a friend."

"Where should we go?" Dario asked.

"Let's go down by the river," Sanja replied. "You can see all the new restaurants and coffee shops that opened near the pedestrian bridge."

"Lead the way."

Dario followed Sanja to one of the outdoor restaurants on the Drava shoreline, near the new Bridge of Youth, and ordered coffee. The iconic nine-hundred-foot pedestrian bridge crosses the river and leads to the Copacabana, the famous recreational center and another Osijek icon.

"Paul told me the bridge was rebuilt after the war, but I had no idea how beautiful it is," Dario said as he admired the structure.

"The pedestrian and bike lights were added in two thousand seven," Sanja replied.

"It's great," Dario said as they had their coffee. "I can't imagine what it was like for you as a nurse during the war."

"It was terrible," Sanja replied. "Dealing with all the injuries and death and not being able to do anything to stop it. And then not having you here made it that much worse."

"You said you understood why I had to leave?"

"At the time, I did. But what I didn't understand was why you didn't come back. We had a plan to go to America together."

"I couldn't come back. I had performing commitments. And you couldn't join me; you're nursing career was here."

"I also thought our relationship was a commitment."

"It was, but we both agreed that to have a long-distance relationship wasn't going to work," Dario said.

"And it didn't," Sanja replied.

"But you need to know that I never stopped loving you," Dario said as he moved close to her and took her hand.

"But now I have someone else who loves me," Sanja replied as she took her hand away.

"Do you love him?"

Sanja paused. "I appreciate him. He's good to me and was here when I needed someone."

"I'm sorry I didn't come back," Dario said.

"Me, too."

"Well, I should get back to the hotel."

"And I need to get home. Thank you for the coffee."

"You're welcome. I'll walk you back to the cab stand," Dario said, and they left the restaurant and got back to the hotel just as a cab pulled up.

"Goodnight," Dario said.

"Goodnight."

Sanja got in the cab and drove off, and Dario walked back to the Royal, thinking about Sanja and the love he lost.

When he walked into the Hotel Royal lobby, a notification bell was next to a sign that read 'ring for service.' Dario rang the bell, and a young man walked out from a back room dressed in a Hotel Royal uniform.

"Yes, sir?"

"Is Mr. Horvat here?"

"No, sir. My name is Henry, the assistant manager. Can I help you?"

"I'm Dario Dimitric, and I'm in room 315. Mr. Horvat is holding a package for me in the hotel safe, and I'd like to get it back."

Henry verified Dario's identity with his passport. "Yes, sir, Mr. Dimitric, just give me a second." He unlocked the safe, found the package, and handed it to Dario.

"Thank you."

"Is there anything else I can do for you?"

"No. Goodnight."

"Goodnight, sir."

Dario walked up the stairs to his room, went inside, and locked the door. As he sat on the bed and opened the package, there was a knock at the door. Dario hid the package in the closet, opened the door, and saw Sanja.

"Sanja?"

"Can I come in?"

"Of course."

Sanja walked in, and Dario checked the hallway to make sure no one saw her, then shut and locked the door.

"Don't worry," Sanja said. "No one saw me come up. There wasn't anyone at the front desk."

"What are you doing here?" he asked.

"I needed to tell you something." Sanja walked over to Dario and gave him a passionate kiss. "I do still love you."

CHAPTER IV

The next morning, after a night of lovemaking, Dario and Sanja were lying in bed.

"I need to go. I'll be late for work," Sanja said as she got out of bed and got dressed.

"When can I see you again?" Dario said as he got out of bed and put on his pants.

"I'll let you know."

They kissed, and Sanja walked to the door to leave.

"Wait," Dario said. "Before you go, I want to show you something."

He took the package out of the closet, opened it and brought the gold bar and ring to Sanja. "These were in the package you gave me from my grandmother."

Sanja looked at the gold bar. "This is a Nazi gold bar from World War Two. Where did your grandmother get it?"

"I don't know. And that's my grandmother's wedding ring. There's an inscription on the inside of the band in German that I can't translate. Can you?"

Sanja looked at the inscription. "It's hard to read, but I think it says, 'The treasure you seek will be found after you die.'

"The treasure you seek will be found after you die? What do you think it means?"

"It sounds like it's referring to the peace and joy we find with God after we die. But you should show these to Father Josip," she said handing the gold bar and ring back to Dario. "Since he was in Osijek with your grandmother during World War Two, I'll bet he can tell you about them."

"That's a great idea. I'll talk to him after church this morning. Will you be there?"

"No, I have to work, but I'll call you later."

"Good."

"Sanja kissed him and left the room.

As Dario, carrying the package containing the gold bar and ring in his sports coat pocket, left his room for church, he met Horvat at the front desk.

"Good morning, Dario."

"Good morning, Mr. Horvat."

"You're up early."

"I'm on my way to church."

"My assistant told me you picked up your package last night."

"That's right."

"Do you want to put it back in the safe?"

"No, I'm going to keep it with me. But thanks."

"Well, enjoy the service."

When Dario got to the church, Emily and Paul were already there sitting in a back pew. "You guys are already here. I'm impressed."

"You can thank me for that," Emily said. "He was trying to get out of coming."

"I'm already good with God," Paul said, smiling.

As Father Josip walked onto the altar, wearing his mass vestments, accompanied by two altar boys, one carrying a cross and the other a *Bible*, everyone stood up and made the sign of the cross. Then Josip took the *Bible* from the altar boy, approached a podium in front of the altar, set it down, and an organist started to play. The congregation, Josip, and the altar boys all sang a hymn, and at the end of the hymn, Josip walked back to the podium.

"Amen," he said, then made the sign of the cross. The congregation repeated his Amen and made the sign of the cross. "Please be seated."

As everyone, including the altar boys, sat down and Josip opened the *Bible,* Dario looked over the crowded church and saw Philip sitting with Vera in a front pew near the altar.

"Before we start the mass this morning," Father Josip said, "I want to take this opportunity to acknowledge the passing of one of our devoted parishioners, Ljubica Kvaternik. Ljubica was a good woman, full of compassion and generosity. And because of what she did for the city of Osijek and many of us here today, she is truly blessed. Her son, Philip, and her grandson, Dario, both members of our congregation, are with us today, and our prayers go out to them in their hour of sorrow. May she rest in peace. Amen."

The mass concluded, and as people left the church, Dario watched his uncle and Vera exit through a side door near the front of the church.

"Emily and I want to take you to Café Mignon for breakfast. You up for it?" Paul asked Dario.

"You're inviting me? Really?"

"I didn't say we were going to pay. We just want to take you there," Paul said, smiling.

"Funny. Listen, you guys go on ahead, and I'll meet you. I need to talk to Father Josip for a minute."

"Don't be long," Emily said. "I'm hungry."

"Me, too," Paul said.

"I'll be there as soon as I can," Dario said and walked to an office near the altar and knocked on the door.

"Come in," Father Josip said from inside the office.

Dario walked into the office and saw Josip sitting at his desk out of his mass vestments.

"Father, can I talk to you?"

"Certainly, Dario. Please sit down."

Dario closed the office door and took a seat in front of the desk.

"What's on your mind?" Josip asked.

"Well, first of all, I want to thank you for the wonderful acknowledgment you gave my grandmother at mass this morning."

"Well, she was a wonderful woman. How are you holding up?"

"I miss her."

"We all do."

"Can I ask you a question?" Dario said.

"Sure."

Dario took the package out of his pocket, unwrapped it and handed the gold bar and ring to Josip. "Before my grandmother died, she gave me these. Do you recognize them?"

"You say your grandmother gave you these?" Josip asked, looking at them.

"Yes. Is there something wrong?"

"It's just that I haven't seen a gold bar like this since World War Two. The Croatians made them for the Nazis."

"But how would my grandmother have gotten it?"

"Your grandmother and I were both teenagers when Hitler came into Croatia and created the Nazi puppet state. So she could have gotten it then."

"Are you saying my grandmother was involved with the Nazis?"

"Not directly, only through her family. Her relative, Slavko Kvaternik, was a general in the Croatian army and a German sympathizer. He supported the evil Ante Pavelic, the Croatian prime minister, and was responsible for starting the Ustasa. Ustasa's goal was to exterminate everyone in the country who wasn't Croatian. Slavko and Pavelic created Jasenovac, a concentration camp they used to kill thousands of Serbs, Jews, and Gypsies. But before they killed them, they took their gold jewelry and made gold bars out of it."

"So, the name Kvaternik is part of Croatian history because of the horrible things my grandmother's family did during World War Two?"

"I'm afraid so. And even though Ljubica hated what Slavko did, she was too young to do anything about it."

"What happened to the gold after the war?"

"The Ustasa used most of it to leave Croatia and go to Latin America and Rome, and the rest remained in Croatia and has never been found."

"Did the Catholic church support the Nazis?"

"Yes. The church got paid handsomely to support the Ustasa movement and hide the Nazi sympathizers after the war."

"And this gold bar must mean my grandmother got some of it."

"It's possible, but if she did, I'm sure she used the money to help the people of Osijek, regardless of their ethnicity."

"She also gave me that ring. Do you recognize it?"

"That was her wedding ring from her second marriage to Hrusto. I performed that ceremony."

"There's a German phrase inside the band that reads, 'The treasure you seek will be found after you die.' What do you think it means?" Dario asked as Josip looked at the inscription.

"Your grandmother was a devoted Catholic," Josip said. "So, it must mean when we die, and our soul is joined with God in heaven, we will be bestowed with his treasures."

"Thank you, Father, you've been very helpful."

"You're welcome, Dario, anytime."

"I probably won't see you again. I'll be heading back to America at the end of this week," Dario said as he re-wrapped the package and put it back in his sport coat pocket.

"Then, have a safe trip and come back to Osijek when you can."

"I will. And thank you again for being such a good friend to my grandmother."

"She was a good friend to me. I'll miss her."

"Goodbye."

After Dario walked out of the office, Josip looked up to heaven and made the sign of the cross.

"Don't worry, Ljubica, your secret's safe with me."

After Dario left Josip's office, he went to Cafe' Mignon to meet Paul and Emily. On the way, he thought about what Josip told him about his family and understood why his grandmother and mother never told him about that part of the Kvaternik family history. When Dario got to the Café, he joined Paul and Emily, sitting at a table.

"How did your meeting with Father Josip go?" Emily asked.

"It was distressing," Dario replied.

"Why? Was it about what your grandmother gave you?" Paul asked.

"Yeah. I'll tell you all about it, but first I need a drink. What are you two having?"

"I ordered a Bambus," Emily said.

"I used to love wine and coke," Dario said. "But I need something stronger, like a shot of Tequila."

"Wow, tequila for breakfast, you are distressed," Paul said.

"You want to join me?" Dario asked Paul.

"Why not, for distress prevention."

After a waitress took their order, Drazen, who was also in the restaurant having breakfast, saw the group and walked over to their table.

"Drazen, it's good to see you," Emily asked.

"You, too," Drazen replied.

"You want to join us for breakfast?" Dario asked.

"Thank you, but I just finished. I came over to say hi to Paul and the beautiful Emily," he said, kissing Emily's hand.

"Thank you, Drazen," Emily said.

"Hey, watch it, buddy; she's married," Paul said, smiling.

"For the moment," Emily replied as she smiled and winked at Drazen. "But stay in touch with me just in case."

"By the way, Dario, your uncle Philip was in the bar last night."

"He was?"

"Yes, he came in with the owner of the assisted living facility your grandmother was in and another big, mean-looking man I've never seen before. Your uncle introduced him as a German real estate investor."

"That must be the guy I saw him with," Paul said.

"Did he say anything else?" Dario asked.

"Just that he and your uncle were business partners and in Osijek to find a property to buy."

"Interesting. Thank you for telling me," Dario said.

"No problem. Now when are you two coming to sing at Vinoteka?" Drazen asked.

"How about tonight? Does that work for you, Paul?" Dario asked.

"Before you answer, you should know drinks will be on the house," Drazen said.

"He'll be there," Emily said.

"Great. Then I'll see you guys tonight at around nine."

As Drazen walked away, Dario looked at Paul.

"That's strange. My uncle doesn't have any real estate experience."

"He must have gotten into it in Germany," Paul said.

"Yeah," Dario replied suspiciously. "Well, thanks for breakfast."

"You're welcome. Sure you don't want another shot of tequila?"

"No, thanks. I've got to meet Vera at the assisted living facility."

"You still haven't told us what your grandmother gave you and why your meeting with Father Josip made you so upset?" Emily asked.

Dario took out the package and handed it to Paul. "Don't let anyone see what's in it."

"Why? What is it, gold or something?" Paul said as he unwrapped it and saw the gold bar and ring. "Holy shit! It is gold."

"Not so loud," Dario said.

"Let me see those," Emily said as she took the gold and ring from Paul. "This looks like one of the gold bars left in Croatia after World War Two, I've read about them. And this is your grandmother's wedding ring?"

"Yes, from her marriage to her second husband, Hrusto."

"Where do you think Ljubica got the gold?" Paul asked.

"Father Josip said that during the war, my grandmother's relative, a man named Slavko Kvaternik, started a pro-Nazi group called Ustasa."

"Slavko Kvaternik, he's the Croatian army General responsible for killing thousands of Serbians and Jews during World War Two," Emily said.

"Yes, and he made these gold bars out of their jewelry."

"And that's how Father Josip thinks your grandmother got it?" Paul asked.

"He didn't know that for sure."

"Did Ljubica ever mention anything to you about having gold?" Emily asked.

"No, but considering her family was wealthy, it makes sense," Dario replied.

"Why do you think she gave you her wedding ring?" Emily asked.

"As a remembrance, I assume. Listen, I have to go," Dario said as he put the re-wrapped package back in his pocket and stood up to leave. "I'll see you tonight at Vinoteka."

"We'll be there," Paul said.

"And be careful," Emily said.

"I will," Dario said and left the restaurant.

As Dario walked back to the Royal, still thinking about his meeting with Josip, Tomo pulled up next to him in his police car and rolled down his window.

"Dario, can I talk to you for a minute?" Tomo asked.

"What's it about?"

"Get in, and I'll tell you."

Dario got in the passenger front seat next to Tomo.

"What's up?" Dario asked.

"I have some information about the fire at your grandmother's house," Tomo said as he took out a small plastic bag and showed it to Dario.

"What is this?" Dario asked.

"It's a cigarette butt we found at your grandmother's house. It indicates someone might have started the fire."

"You mean on purpose?" But why?" Dario asked.

"We think they were looking for something in the house and set the fire to cover their tracks," Tomo replied.

"What were they looking for?" Dario asked.

"I was hoping you might know."

Not wanting to tell Tomo about the gold, Dario paused.

"I don't have any idea. My grandmother didn't tell me about hiding anything of value in the house."

"Would she have told anyone else? Like her son Philip?" Tomo asked.

"I don't think so. My grandmother and my uncle weren't on the best of terms."

"Are you familiar with that brand of cigarette?"

Dario looked at the cigarette butt and saw the word Pueblo stenciled around the filter.

"It says the brand is Pueblo, but I'm not a smoker, so it doesn't mean anything to me."

"Pueblo is a German cigarette maker. Do you know anyone who smokes that brand?"

"No."

"At your grandmother's wake, Sanja told you she had something to give you from your grandmother," Tomo said.

"That's right."

"And you were going to the hospital to pick it up. Did you?".

"Yes, but I'm sure you already knew that," Dario replied, assuming Sanja must have told Tomo he came to see her.

"You want to tell me what your grandmother gave you?"

"She gave me her wedding ring as a remembrance."

"And that's all? Just a ring?" Tomo asked.

"Yes. Is there anything else? I've got an appointment to keep."

"There's one more thing. The assisted living facility your grandmother was in has been under investigation for the past several months."

"Why?"

"Since Vera Juric bought the place, several residents have passed away. And most of them from heart attacks."

"That's how my grandmother died. Is Vera responsible?"

"The investigation hasn't turned up anything concrete yet, but I thought you should know."

"I appreciate it," Dario replied.

"If you find out who smokes that brand of cigarette, let me know," Tomo said.

"I will. And you do the same," Dario said and got out of the car.

As he walked back to the Royal, Dario thought about the fire and the German cigarette butt and remembered Philip's real estate partner.

"I need to find out who that German guy is," Dario said

CHAPTER V

When Dario got back to the Royal, there was a policeman parked in front of the hotel. Assuming Tomo was having him followed, Dario walked into the hotel and up to the reception desk as Horvat finished with another guest.

"Hi, Dario, just coming back from church?" Horvat asked.

"From breakfast at Café Mignon."

"That's one of my favorite places."

"Mine, too," Dario said as he walked up the stairs to his room.

When he got into his room, he locked the door, put the gold and ring back in the closet, then walked onto the balcony and saw the police car still parked in front of the hotel. Needing to go to the assisted living facility and not wanting to be followed, Dario put on a sweatshirt and cap to cover his face and walked out of the hotel into the Korzo.

As he walked, Dario looked back and saw the policeman following him. He picked his pace, and when he got to Café Mignon, he went inside, hid in the men's room, and waited for the policeman to pass the restaurant. Then Dario left the restaurant, got on the tram and went to Dom Sunce.

The Dom Sunce facility was built in 2017 and is located just outside Osijek near the Drava. When Dario arrived at the facility, an older nurse standing at a reception desk greeted him.

"Can I help you, sir?" she said.

"I'm here to see Vera Juric."

"Your name?"

"Dario Dimitric."

"One moment."

The woman picked up a telephone and dialed a number.

"Miss Juric, there's a gentleman named Dario Dimitric here to see you. Yes, ma'am."

The woman hung up the phone. "She's finishing a meeting and will be with you in a few minutes. You're welcome to wait for her in the reception area."

"Thank you."

Dario sat in the reception area near the desk and picked up one of the facility's marketing brochures. According to the brochure, the one-story facility had thirty-one-bedroom apartments and twenty-four-hour nursing care. From what Dario could see from the reception area, the facility was clean and well maintained.

While Dario waited, he saw several older female residents supporting themselves with walkers accompanied by nurses walk past the reception area and down a hallway. As Dario watched them clutch their walkers for support, he thought about his grandmother. The last time Dario saw her, she was healthy and strong and moved around better than women half her age. But now, seeing the weakened condition of the other women, he wondered if before his grandmother died, she lost the ability to walk on her own and needed help. And it made him sad he wasn't there to take care of her.

A couple of minutes later, Vera, dressed in a business suit, walked into the reception area, over to Dario, and shook his hand.

"Dario, it's good to see you again. How are you doing since the funeral?"

"I'm fine. Still can't believe my grandmother's gone."

"I know. I hear that a lot in my business. You have my sincere condolences. Everyone here loved your grandmother and was so sorry she died. Come on. I'll take you to her apartment."

Dario followed Vera out of the reception area and down the hallway. As they passed a cafeteria, Dario watched Vera greet several of the residents, and it was apparent they liked her and showed no signs of mistreatment or animosity.

"We have a full-time chef on staff, and the tenants can request pretty much anything they want to eat. They can also cook for themselves in their apartments if they prefer."

"Did my grandmother cook?"

"Absolutely, she cooked all the time."

Dario smiled as he remembered all the delicious Croatian dishes his grandmother would make for him. They continued down the hall, passing nurses and orderlies tending to various residents, and stopped in front of an apartment.

"This is where your grandmother stayed," Vera said as she unlocked the apartment and walked inside.

Dario followed her into the apartment, and while Vera turned on the lights and opened the curtains, he looked around. The apartment was small and furnished with a T.V., a single bed, a couch, a dresser, two end tables, two lamps, and a small table with two chairs near a kitchenette.

"Was my grandmother in her apartment when she had her heart attack?" Dario asked.

"Yes. She didn't come to breakfast that morning, and one of the orderlies went to check on her. He found her passed out on the floor and did CPR, but it was no use."

"Was she complaining about chest pains before her heart attack?"

"No. But as you know, your grandmother was a private woman and may have decided not to tell us."

"So, how do you know it was a heart attack? Did you do an autopsy?"

"No. Your uncle said there was no reason. He was comfortable with our assessment."

"Can I see my grandmother's medical records?"

"I'm sorry, but I can't show those to you without your uncle's permission. Since he is the only surviving direct descendant, he has total control of his mother's information."

"Then I'll talk to him about it."

"Well, now that you've seen the facility and the kind of care we give, is there anything else I can help you with?" Vera asked.

"Just one thing. I know there were family photos hung in the living room of my grandmother's house that weren't destroyed in the fire."

"That's right. There were three that survived."

"And you have them?"

The Picture Box

"I do."

"They're important to me, so can I buy them from you?"

Vera paused for a moment before she answered. "Since your uncle doesn't want them, you can have them. And there's no charge."

"Thank you."

"They're in our storage room, so on your way out, I'll get them. Now since I've done something for you, I want to ask you a question."

"Sure."

"When a resident checks in to the facility, we record all the belongings they bring with them. And when your grandmother came in, she was wearing a gold wedding band that we can't seem to find. I don't suppose you know anything about it?"

"Ah, no, I assumed she had it on when she was buried."

Realizing Dario wasn't going to tell her anything, Vera ended the conversation.

"Fine. Well, let's get those pictures, "Vera said and escorted Dario back to the reception area. "Wait here."

Dario sat down again, still thinking about the autopsy, and a minute later, Vera returned carrying a medium-sized sealed package.

"All three of the pictures are in here," she said as she handed the package to Dario.

"Thank you for the pictures and for letting me see my grandmother's room," he said.

"You're welcome. And I hope you feel better about how we treated your grandmother before she died?"

Dario forced a smile. "Yes, I do. Goodbye."

"Goodbye," Vera replied.

Dario returned to the Royal, and the police car was gone. He brought the package of pictures to his room and opened it. Inside were three twenty-four by twenty-four photos mounted in hand-carved wood frames. Each image had a metal plate etched with the name 'Varnai Photography Studio' and reminded Dario that he needed to pick up the negative and the rest of his grandmother's photos.

The first photo was of a ten-year-old Dario standing with Blanka and Nikola, in their forties, and Ljubica in her sixties, in front of the Cathedral on Ponoc'ka, the Croatian celebration of Christmas Eve. They each held a glass of wine as they waited to go into the church for midnight mass.

Taken in December, the photo showed Osijek covered in a beautiful, thick blanket of snow and made Dario remember how much fun he and Paul would have in the winter, grabbing onto passing cars' back bumpers and being pulled down the snow-covered streets. While the picture brought back happy memories of sharing those holy days with his family, it also made Dario sad to know all the people in the photo he loved so much were now gone. Overcome with melancholy, Dario kissed each of their photo faces.

"I know we'll all be together again," he said and set the picture down.

The next picture was of a fifteen-year-old Dario and a forty-five-year-old Blanka swimming at his grandmother's vacation home on the Adriatic. Like the first photo, the image brought back beautiful memories of Osijek's peaceful summer days before the war and the fun he had with his mother and grandmother.

The Picture Box

The final photo was of Ljubica standing with Dario in front of the Hotel Royal on the day he left for America. Ljubica, now in her seventies, and the eighteen-year-old Dario, are hugging. While Dario was embarking on a trip that would make his singing dreams come true, he had no idea it would be the last time he would see his grandmother alive.

"I'll never forget what you did for me, Grandmother. I love you."

Dario rewrapped the photos and put them in the closet with the gold and ring. Then he got ready to meet Paul and Emily at Vinoteka. But before he left the room, there was a knock at the door, and he opened it to find Horvat.

"Mr. Horvat, can I help you with something?"

"I didn't see you come back to the hotel."

"I just got back. Is there something you need?"

"While you were out, a policeman came to see you. Is everything okay?"

"Yes. The police are investigating a fire at my grandmother's house. I've already talked to them, but they must have additional questions. How long was the policeman here?"

"About an hour, he got called back to police headquarters but said he'd be back."

"Well, thank you for telling me. I've got to go out, but I'll be back in a couple of hours."

"One more thing. Father Josip called and left a message for you to call him," Horvat said and handed Dario Josip's telephone number.

"Thank you," Dario said, and Horvat walked away.

After Horvat was gone, Dario took out his cell phone and called Father Josip.

"Hello, Father, I got your message. Is there something you need? He did? When? What did he want? I can't come to see you tonight, but I'll come first thing tomorrow morning if that works? Great. See you then. Goodnight."

Dario hung up the call and left the room.

When Dario got to Vinoteka, Paul and Emily were sitting at the bar with Drazen having a drink. The place was full of people waiting for the show.

"Quite a turnout," Dario said.

"I sent emails to all my customers telling them you were back and to come to the restaurant tonight to hear a real Las Vegas performer," Drazen said.

"What about me? Paul asked.

"Oh yeah, and you too," Drazen replied, laughing. "So, what are you guys going to sing?"

"I think we should start with *Da iman bijeli cadilak*," Dario said.

"*If I had a white Cadillac,*" that is a great song," Emily said.

"And then we can sing Tamara by Boris Nokovic', Paul said.

"Those are both great. Are you ready?" Drazen asked.

"Just about," Paul said as he gulped down the rest of his drink. "Now I'm ready."

As the men walked up to the stage with Drazen, the audience erupted with clapping and cheering, and Drazen approached one of the microphones.

The Picture Box

"Welcome all to an extraordinary Vinoteka event." The audience clapped and cheered again.

"Tonight Vinoteka is proud to have two of our favorite singers back after several years to perform. The last time they sang here together was twenty years ago, and during that time, Dario went to America to sing and is now headlining a show in Las Vegas." The audience clapped and cheered. "So, let's give a warm Vinoteka welcome back to Dario Dimitric and Paul Novak."

The audience clapped and cheered again as Drazen left the stage, and Dario walked up to the microphone. "Thank you. It's a real pleasure for us to be here tonight to share some of our favorite Croatian music. We hope you enjoy it."

"And if you don't, keep it to yourselves," Paul joked,

The audience laughed, and Dario and Paul started to sing.

While Dario and Paul sang at Vinoteka, Sanja was making her rounds at the hospital. One of the rooms she checked contained a little boy and girl hooked to I.Vs.

"How are you both tonight?" Sanja asked as she checked their charts.

"I don't feel good," the little girl said.

"Me either," said the little boy.

"I know. You'll feel better after your treatments," Sanja said.

"Promise?" the little girl asked.

"Yeah, you promise?" the boy asked.

"Promise," Sanja said as she gave both of them a kiss. "Now, get some sleep, and I'll see you in the morning. Goodnight."

"Goodnight," Dario said, and Sanja left.

As she walked into the hallway, Schmidt, wearing a medical lab coat and carrying a clipboard, approached her.

"Excuse me," he said. "Yes?"

"Are you Sanja Babic, the supervising nurse in this ward?" Schmidt said.

"That's right?

"My name is Doctor Karl Schmidt, and I'm a visiting German geriatric expert hired by the Croatian government to assess the care given to seniors at the Dom Sunce assisted living facility here in Osijek."

"How can I help you, Doctor Schmidt?"

"The facility's visitor records indicate that you were at the facility recently visiting Ljubica Kvaternik, an eighty-five-year-old woman who died of a heart attack. Is that right?"

"Yes."

"I'm talking to people who visited the facility to get their impression of the care the facility provided. Can I ask you a few questions?"

"Okay."

"What was your relationship to the patient?"

"She was a friend."

"Did she say anything about the care the facility provided while she was there?"

"She told me the care she received was good but that she didn't like having to be there. Her house burned down, and her son had her move in to be taken care of and not be alone."

"Did she say anything about the check-in process at the facility?"

"What do you mean?"

"The assisted living facility is supposed to keep a record of all the belongings a resident brings with them when they check into the facility. It's Croatian law. Did she say anything about that?"

"What does that have to do with the care she got?"

"Assisted living facility workers are notorious for not recording all the possessions a resident brings with them so they can steal things. And staff honesty at this facility is one of the things I'm focused on," Schmidt replied.

"I understand."

"The possession records indicate that besides Miss Kvaternik's clothing when she checked in, she was wearing a gold wedding ring, but when she passed away, the ring was missing."

"And you think an employee at the facility stole it?" Sanja asked.

"That's what I'm trying to determine. Do you remember Ljubica wearing the ring when you visited?"

"Yes. she never took it off," Sanja replied.

"That's interesting," Schmidt replied. "Did Ljubica say anything about giving it to someone?"

Schmidt's interest in Ljubica's ring, makes Sanja suspicious. "And you say you're working with the Croatian government?" Sanja asked.

"That's right."

"Do you have identification?"

"Certainly."

As Schmidt reaches into his suit jacket for his gun, another nurse comes out of a nearby room.

"Sanja, I need some help," the nurse said.

"Well, I've told you everything I know, Doctor, and I've got to finish my rounds," Sanja said and walked away.

Schmidt watched her go into the room, then threw the clipboard in a nearby trash can and left.

After their performance, Dario and Paul stayed at the bar and had a drink with Drazen.

"You guys were great," Drazen said.

"Thank you," Dario replied.

"You have to come back and sing again, but don't wait so long."

"He won't," Paul replied. "I won't let him."

"And you come and see me in Las Vegas," Dario said as he hugged Drazen.

"Don't be surprised if I do," Drazen said. "Have a safe flight back."

Dario and Paul left the bar and found Sanja waiting outside.

"Hi, Sanja," Paul said. "You missed our show."

"I had to work," Sanja replied. "But I'll bet it was great. Dario, can I talk to you for a minute?"

"Sure," Dario replied.

"I'll see you later, Dario. Goodnight, Sanja," Paul said as he walked away.

"Goodnight," Sanja replied.

"Is everything okay? Dario asked.

"No," Sanja said as she and Dario walked away from the bar.

"What's going on?"

"I got a visit at the hospital from a German doctor asking about your grandmother's wedding ring."

"What are you talking about?"

"His name was Karl Schmidt, and he said he's working for the Croatian government investigating the treatment standards and security at the Dom Sonce assisted living facility. He knew I visited Ljubica and told me the wedding ring she had on when she checked into the facility was missing and wanted to know if I knew anything about it."

"He was German?"

"Yes. And was a big, scary-looking guy."

"What did you tell him?"

"That Ljubica was a friend, and when I visited her, she was wearing the ring, and I didn't know anything about it missing. He's not a German doctor, is he?"

"No, he's my uncle's business partner pretending to be a doctor, and that's how he knows about the ring."

"That means he knows about the gold, too," Sanja said. "And that I'm the one who gave them to you."

"Did you tell Tomo about the doctor coming to see you?" Dario asked.

"Yes. And I told him the doctor was asking about Ljubica's ring."

"Then I'm sure Tomo will be coming to see me," Dario said.

"Please be careful," Sanja said.

"I will," Dario said as he kissed her and walked away.

CHAPTER VI

The following morning, Dario went to the Cathedral to see Father Josip in his office.

"Thank you for coming, Dario."

"On the phone, you said my uncle came to see you yesterday."

"That's right. He knew you came to see me about the gold bar and wedding ring."

"How?"

"He didn't say. He wanted to know if you said anything about Ljubica giving you more than the one bar of gold. And said he owes a lot of money to the German mafia, and if he can't pay it back, the guy he's with will kill him."

"Did he say anything else?"

"No. When I told him you didn't say anything about having more gold, he got angry and left."

"Thank you for telling me, Father," Dario said and started to leave.

"Be careful, Dario, he's desperate."

"I will."

When he got back to the Royal, Tomo's police car was parked out front. Dario went into the hotel and saw Horvat at the reception desk.

"Dario, can I have a word with you? Horvat asked.

"Certainly. What is it?"

"Chief Babic is waiting in your room to see you."

"He must be here with information about the fire. I better get up there," Dario said, then walked up to his room and went inside.

Unknown to Dario, Horvat followed him, stood outside his room, and listened to the door.

"Why are we out here?" Dario asked.

"I want to make sure nobody hears us," Tomo replied. "Now. You were saying?"

"I talked to Sanja, and she told me about the German doctor coming to see her at the hospital about my grandmother's missing ring."

"He's not a German doctor. His name is Karl Schmit, and he's a gangster," Tomo said.

"I know," Dario replied. "My uncle told Father Josip about him, and Father Josip told me."

"I did background check on Schmidt and found out he's a convicted felon working for the German Mafia. And not here looking for your grandmother's wedding ring. But you know that too, don't you?"

Before Dario answered, he went back inside his room, got the gold bar and brought it to Tomo.

"That's why my uncle and Schmidt are here. My grandmother gave me that gold bar and my uncle knows I have it, and thinks I have more that he can use to pay Schmidt for a gambling debt."

Tomo looked at the bar. "Do you have any idea where your grandmother got this?"

"My grandmother's family was working with the Germans in Croatia during World War Two, and that's how I think she got it."

"Did she tell you she had more?"

"No. All I know about is the one bar."

"How do you think your uncle knew you had it?"

"I don't know."

"Who else besides Father Josip and Sanja did you show it to?"

"Sanja told you she saw it?"

"No, she just told me about the ring, but I figured she must have given you something else. Did anyone else see it?"

"Just Paul and Emily," Dario replied.

"What did you do with it after you picked it up from Sanja?"

"I brought it back to the Royal and had Mr. Horvat put it in the hotel safe."

"Horvat, of course," Tomo said.

"You think Horvat saw it and told my uncle?"

"He's the only one who could have. He must have opened the package."

"But why would he do it?"

"He was a Nazi sympathizer during World War Two and a friend of Pero, your grandfather. Pero must have told

Horvat that your grandmother's wealth came from the gold left in Croatia and that she had more of it here in Osijek."

"That's what Schmidt and my uncle were looking for at my grandmother's house. So, what do we do now?" Dario asked.

"Well, since Schmidt and your uncle know you have the gold, they'll assume you know where there's more and come after you. I'm surprised they haven't already."

"Why don't you arrest them?"

"I can't; they haven't done anything illegal."

"What about burning down my grandmother's house?"

"We can't prove the cigarette butt belongs to Schmidt."

"So, what are you going to do? Let them kill me?"

"No, I have a plan. I want Horvat to think your grandmother left you more gold and tell your uncle so they will come after you."

"At the hotel?" Dario asked.

"No, it's too public. Schmidt's too smart for that. We want to force them to confront you in a secluded place that we can control."

"Where?"

"The Osijek catacombs. It's filled with hidden bunkers where you can position yourself. And when Schmidt and Philip come after you, I'll arrest them."

"So, you want them to know where I am?"

"Yes, but don't worry, we'll get them before anything happens to you."

"How will you know which bunker I'm in at the catacombs?"

"As soon as you get to the park and get situated, you'll call me on my cell phone. But just in case take this," Tomo said as he handed Dario a gun.

"Why do I need a gun? I thought you were going to protect me?"

"Like I said, just in case. You going to be okay?"

"As long as I'm alive when it's over, I'll be fine."

"Come on, let's set the trap."

Dario and Tomo walked back into the room, stood close to the room door and Tomo mimed for Dario to follow his lead.

"Thank you, Dario," Tomo said loudly. "I have to go. Enjoy the catacombs tomorrow."

"I will," Dario replied.

Before Tomo could leave the room, Horvat hurried back to the reception desk.

"Goodnight, Mr. Horvat," Tomo said as he walked out of the hotel.

"Goodnight, Chief."

After Horvat watched Tomo leave the hotel, he went back to Dario's room and knocked on the door.

"Who's there?" Dario asked. "Mr. Horvat."

"Just a minute, I'm on the phone," Dario replied, pretending to be talking.

"That's right, Paul, Tomo found another letter addressed to me in my grandmother's house. In the letter, my grandmother said she hid more gold in a bunker at the Osijek catacombs. Right. I'm going there tomorrow morning when the park opens to get it. No, it's better if I go by myself. I'll talk to you when I get back to the hotel. Goodbye," Dario said and opened the door.

"Is there something you need, Mr. Horat?"

"I saw Chief Babic leave and wanted to make sure you're okay," Horvat replied.

"I'm fine. As I said, Tomo came to see me about the fire."

"Any new developments?"

"No, still investigating."

"Well, goodnight," Horvat said.

"Goodnight," Dario replied and shut the door.

The next morning, Dario passed Horvat at the front desk on his way out of the hotel.

"Good morning, Dario," Horvat said. "Going out?"

"Yes, I've got an appointment. See you later."

"Have a good day," Horvat replied.

The Osijek catacombs are within walking distance from the Royal across the pedestrian bridge. The Croatians initially built the eighteenth-century fortress of bunkers and tunnels to store ammunition for potential future wars, but today they're used for concerts and special events.

On his way to the catacombs, Dario thought about the times he would go to there to see shows with his family and friends. But this time, Dario wasn't going for fun. He was going to confront his uncle for putting his grandmother in the assisted living facility to die and for bringing a killer to Osijek. A killer who not only destroyed his grandmother's house and was possibly responsible for her death but was ready to kill him for a single piece of gold. As a combination of fear and anger came over Dario, he gripped the gun Tomo gave him and said a prayer that everything would go according to Tomo's plan and that he wouldn't be killed.

When Dario got to the catacombs, the park was already open and crowded. He took a position in one of the empty bunkers near the park entrance with a clear view of everyone coming into the park—and tried to call Tomo on his cellphone.

"Hello, Tomo, it's Dario, can you hear me? Tomo".

Unable to get a signal, Dario stepped out of the bunker to get better reception as Philip and Schmidt, smoking a cigarette, walked into the park and saw him. Dario ducked back into the bunker and tried to call Tomo again. Still unable to get a signal, Dario moved deeper into the bunker just as Philip and Schmidt walked in.

"Are you sure you saw him go in here?" Philip asked Schmidt.

"Yeah, he's in here somewhere," Schmidt replied as he took out his gun. "You take one side, and I'll take the other."

As Philip walked deeper into the bunker, Dario came out of hiding, jumped him, and knocked him to the ground. As they started to fight, Schmidt walked over and pointed his gun at Dario.

"Stand up and give me your cellphone," Schmidt said to Dario throwing his cigarette butt on the ground.

As Dario stood up, he discreetly picked up Schmidt's cigarette butt and put it in his pocket. "You must be 'Doctor' Karl Schmidt, the German hitman who intentionally burned down my grandmother's house," Dario said as he handed Schmidt his cellphone.

"That's right," Schmidt replied as he threw Dario's cellphone on the ground and stomped on it.

"What do you mean?" Philip said, looking at Schmidt. "You told me the fire at my mother's house was an accident."

"When you couldn't get your mother to tell you where the gold is, I started the fire to give her some encouragement."

"That's why you had me put her in assisted living, so you could force her to tell you about the gold, which means Vera must be involved."

"You just figured that out?" Schmidt replied.

"Why are you guys here? What do you want?" Dario asked.

"You know what we want," Schmidt said. "We're here to get the rest of the gold his mother hid here."

"I don't know what you're talking about," Dario said.

"Cut the shit. We know about the letter you got from your grandmother saying she hid more gold in the catacombs."

"I don't know about any gold," Dario replied. "I'm just here as a tourist."

"That's too bad. Because if you don't know where the gold is, there's no reason to keep you alive," Schmidt said as he cocked the trigger on his gun and prepared to shoot Dario.

Before Schmidt fired, Philip stopped him. "Wait, what if he's telling the truth?"

"He's lying," Schmidt said as he aimed at Dario. "He knows where it is and I'm going to make sure he tells us."

"Go ahead, shoot, Dario said. "The sound will reverberate through the bunker, and everyone in the park will hear it."

"He's right," Philip said.

"Then we'll have to go deeper in the bunker," Schmidt said as he put the barrel of the gun in Dario's back, shoved him deeper into the tunnel, and then shot him in the shoulder.

As Dario yelled out in pain, Schmidt cocked the trigger again.

"The next shot won't be at your shoulder," Schmidt said. "Now, where is the gold?"

"Wait," Dario said. "I'll tell you. It's at the back of the bunker."

"Take us to it."

Dario walked deeper into the bunker, and Schmidt and Philip followed him.

"Where is it?" Schmidt asked.

"It's supposed to be here. I need to look at the letter again to make sure," Dario said as he reached in his pocket, pulled out his gun and shot Schmidt in the side. As Schmidt dropped his gun and fell to the ground, Dario picked up the gun and pointed it at Philip.

"No, please don't shoot me. Getting the gold was all Schmidt's idea," Philip said.

"Bullshit, you and Horvat were in on it, too. Now get your friend up, and let's go. The police want to talk to you."

Philip helped Schmidt to his feet, and Dario escorted them out of the bunker at gunpoint just as Tomo and several police officers showed up.

"Are you okay?" Tomo asked Dario looking at his shoulder.

"Yeah, no thanks to you."

"You didn't call me," Tomo said.

"I tried to call, but I couldn't get a signal. How did you know where I was?"

"We brought Horvat in for questioning and he told us Schmidt and Philip were on their way here. Come on, let's get you to the hospital to have that shoulder looked at. I'm sure Sanja, will be happy you weren't killed."

"If you hadn't given me the gun, I might have been."

"You're welcome," Tomo replied.

Dario reached into his pocket, took out the cigarette butt, and handed it to Tomo.

"What's this?"

"The proof that Schmidt started the fire at my grandmother's house. You're welcome."

CHAPTER VII

When Dario and Tomo got to Osijek Hospital's emergency room, Sanja and an emergency doctor met them and examined Dario.

"It's just a flesh wound," the Doctor said, "You'll be fine. Nurse Babic will dress it, and you can leave."

"Thanks, Doctor," Tomo said.

"Yeah, thanks," Dario said.

"Let's get you fixed up," Sanja said and started to take Dario into an examination room.

At that moment, Tomo got a call on his walkie-talkie.

"Captain Babic, come in. Over."

"This is Babic," Tomo replied.

"Sir, we just got word that there's another death at the Dom Sonce assistant living facility. Over."

"Send a couple of officers and an ambulance to the facility, and I'll meet them there. Over and out."

"I want to go with you," Dario said.

"Not until I bandage your shoulder," Sanja said.

"She's right, Dario. You get taken of, and I'll send an officer to pick you up. Is that okay with you, Nurse?"

Yes, Captain. And you be careful, too," Sanja replied.

"I will. I'll call you later," Tomo said and left the hospital.

Sanja took Dario into an examination room, had him sit on an examination table, and removed his shirt.

"So, you want to tell me what happened?" Sanja asked while she dressed Dario's wound.

"Karl Schmidt, the fake German doctor, turned out to be a German mafia hitman. He and my uncle came after me for the additional gold they thought I had, and Schmidt shot me. And I shot him."

"Is he dead?"

"He wasn't the last time I saw him."

"And Philip?"

"Tomo arrested him, too."

"You're lucky to be alive," Sanja said as she finished bandaging Dario's shoulder, and he put his shirt back on.

"I know."

"This wound will take quite a while to heal, so be careful and have it looked at when you get back to Vegas. Goodbye," Sanja said and started to walk out of the examination room.

"Wait," Dario said and walked over to her. "Can I see you again before I leave?"

"No. I love you, but you're going back to America, and I'm staying here. And I can't risk losing my relationship with Tomo. He's my husband, and I won't do anything to hurt him."

"Me either. Can we stay friends?" Dario asked.

"Always," Sanja replied and kissed him. "Goodbye."

"Goodbye."

As Sanja and Dario walked out of the examination room, a police officer walked into the emergency room.

"Mr. Dimitric?"

"Yes."

"I'm here to take you to Dom Sunce to meet with Captain Babic," the officer said.

"Let's go," Dario replied.

When Dario got to Dom Sunce, he saw two ambulance attendants bring a sheet-covered body out of the facility and put it in a waiting ambulance.

"Where's Captain Babic?" Dario asked one of the officers.

"He's inside talking to the owner of the facility," the officer replied.

"Thanks," Dario said, then walked into the facility and saw Tomo and two other policemen escorting a handcuffed Vera.

Dario watched the officers put Vera into a squad car and then approached Tomo.

"What's going on?"

"We're taking Vera back to police headquarters for questioning concerning the death of several residents, including your grandmother. We have proof Vera murdered them so she could take their assets."

"How do you know that?"

"I told you about the investigation, but I didn't tell you that after your grandmother died, I put an undercover nurse in the facility and she found out the deaths weren't caused by heart attacks, they were poisoned. That's why Vera would have their bodies buried without an autopsy, so she could take their assets without anyone knowing the truth."

"Are you saying my grandmother was murdered?" Dario asked.

"We won't know for sure until we have this latest victim autopsied. If we find poison, we'll need to exhume Ljubica's body and have it tested. Are you okay with that?"

"I'm sure my grandmother would want it done to prove Vera is a killer. What about my uncle? He was the one who didn't want an autopsy performed on my grandmother. Do you think he's involved?"

"There's no evidence he knew anything about the poisonings, but we think Schmidt did and blackmailed Vera to give him a piece of the action."

"So, what happens now?" Dario asked.

"I'll set up the autopsies and let you know what we find," Tomo said. "Come on. I'll give you a ride back to the Royal."

"Thanks."

When Dario got back to the hotel, the assistant manager was at the front desk.

"Hi, Mr. Dimitric."

"Hi, Henry. Where's Mr. Horvat?"

"I was told he's taking a few days off. Is there something I can do for you?"

"I'll be checking out tomorrow morning, and I'd like to have some pictures shipped to Las Vegas. Can you do that?"

"No, sir. But I'm sure Varnai, the photography store, could do it," Henry said.

"That's a good idea. I need to go there anyway. Thank you," Dario said.

Dario went up to his room, picked up the three wrapped photos, and took them to Varnai. When he got to the studio, Meric was working with a client.

"Dario, it's good to see you again. I was hoping you'd hadn't forgotten to come in," Meric said.

"Am I interrupting anything?" Dario asked.

"No," Meric replied. "Just let me finish with this customer."

While Meric finished with the customer, Dario looked around the shop at the pictures Meric had displayed on the walls. There were pictures of several memorable Osijek landmarks; the Cathedral, the Hotel Royal, the electric tram, the Korzo and several of the shops, the Drava River, the Adriatric Sea and various Osijek families. As Dario looked at the photos, he couldn't help but feel both sadness and pride. Sadness because he would never be in Osijek with his grandmother and parents again, and pride because of how beautiful the city is and how much he and his family loved it.

When Meric finished with the customer, he closed the shop and approached Dario.

"Now, what have you got there?" Meric asked Dario as he pointed to the package Dario brought.

"I have three family photos my grandmother had in her house, and I want to see if you can ship them back to Vegas for me."

"Certainly. Let me take a look."

Dario unwrapped the pictures, and Meric looked at them.

"I remember these pictures," Meric said. "These were your grandmother's favorites. Especially this one."

As Meric picked up the photo of Dario and Ljubica standing in front of the Hotel Royal the day Dario left for America, there was a knock at the shop door.

"Excuse me," Meric said to Dario, then opened the door, and Father Josip walked in.

"Dario, it's good to see you," Josip said.

"You, too, Father."

"I wanted Father Josip to meet us here so that we could talk with you," Meric said to Dario.

"About what?"

"About these," Meric said as he took a small wooden box from under a counter and opened it. "Remember I told you your grandmother had me develop some pictures that she forgot to pick up?"

"Yes," Dario replied.

"These are those."

Meric took out several small black and white photos. "Look at them," he said to Dario.

Dario looked at one of the pictures and saw a teenage girl and boy standing next to a German soldier in uniform, each with a shovel digging a hole. And next to the hole was a pile of gold bars like the one Dario got from his grandmother.

"Who are the kids in the picture, and what is the soldier doing?" Dario asked.

"That's your grandmother and me here in Osijek during World War Two," Father Josip said. "And the soldier is making us bury gold."

"Who took the picture?"

"Another soldier. Then he gave the camera to your grandmother to hold and forgot it," Josip said.

"How did you get it?" Dario asked Meric.

"Ljubica gave it to me and asked me to develop the pictures and keep them safe."

"So, you and my grandmother knew where the gold was?" Dario asked Josip.

"No. Like I told you, the Ustasa used most of it to leave the country," Josip replied. "And the rest is still in Croatia somewhere."

"Then if her wealth didn't come from gold, where did it come from?" Dario asked.

"Look at the rest of the pictures," Meric said to Dario. "Those are pictures Ljubica had me take at the Royal when she was the manager during World War Two. The Nazis would go to the Royal to celebrate their victories and show the priceless paintings Hitler stole during his conquests."

"I don't understand," Dario said. "Why was my grandmother having you take pictures of paintings?"

"You want to answer that, Father?" Meric said to Josip.

"After the celebrations were over and the Nazis left Osijek, Ljubica would store some of the paintings at the hotel, and use the photos to keep track of which ones she had," Josip said.

"But after some of the celebrations, there were some paintings she didn't store at the hotel," Meric said. "She would give them to me, and I would sell them for her on the black market."

"Are you saying my grandmother stole priceless paintings from Hitler?" Dario asked.

"That's right, and she used the money to help the surviving family members of the Jews and Serbs the Ustasa killed in World War Two. And I was one of them." Meric said.

"She felt by taking some of the paintings back from Hitler, selling them and using the money for good, she was in some small way making up for his atrocities. And Mr. Meric and I helped her to do it," Josip replied.

"Where would she hide the paintings she stole until you could sell them?" Dario asked.

"I'll show you," Meric replied.

Meric cut the paper backing off the photo of Dario and his grandmother and revealed a painting underneath.

"That is an original Da Vinci print entitled Lady with an Ermine," Meric said. "He painted it in 1489, and it's one of his most famous. The subject of the painting was Cecilia Gallerani, the Duke of Milan's mistress. It's one of only four portraits Da Vinci did, and Hitler stole it from the Italians. And with the money from this painting, we'll be able to continue your grandmother's charitable work."

"Are there other paintings under the other two photos?" Dario asked.

"No, this is the last one. Ljubica was going to bring it to me before she died," Meric said.

"This is unbelievable," Dario said as he looked at the painting.

"Your grandmother helped so many people through the years. You should be proud of her," Father Josip said.

"I am. More than you know," Dario replied. "Thank you both for being her friends, and I hope I'll see you both again."

"God willing, we'll be here," Meric said. "And I'll ship these pictures to Vegas for you, along with the picture box and your baby picture."

"Thank you," Dario said as he started to leave the shop and then stopped. "Oh, you both should know that Captain Babic arrested Philip, his German partner, and the owner of the assisted living facility. But I'm sure he'll tell you about it," he said and walked out of the shop. "Goodbye."

The following day, Paul came to the Royal to pick Dario up and take him to the airport. As they loaded Dario's luggage in Paul's car, Tomo drove up in his police car and got out.

"I came to say goodbye, Dario," Tomo said. "And to tell you, the last victim we autopsied was poisoned. Which means we'll need to exhume Ljubica's body and test it."

"I understand," Dario replied.

"But don't worry, I'll have Father Josip oversee her reburial."

"Thank you."

"And it also means we're charging both Vera and Schmidt with murder and will try them here in Croatia."

"And my uncle?"

"He's being extradited back to Germany to the authorities there.

"Thanks for everything," Dario said and shook Tomo's hand.

"Does this mean you don't think I'm the class jerk anymore?" Tomo asked.

"I wouldn't go that far," Dario replied, smiling. "Come back soon," Tomo said.

"I will," Dario said as he got in Paul's car and they drove off.

"Listen, Paul, before we go to the airport, I'd like to go back to St. Anas and say goodbye to my grandmother."

"No problem," Paul said.

When they got to the graveyard, Paul stayed in the car.

"I'll wait here. Say goodbye to grandma for me," he said.

"I will," Dario said and walked to Ljubica's grave.

"I know about everything you did for the people of Osijek, Grandmother, and I love you for it. And I want to thank you for the gold bar and your wedding ring. I'm wearing it around my neck and will never take it off."

Dario walked over to Hrusto's grave and found the metal flower receptacle near his headstone tipped over and lying on the ground.

"Even though we never met, Hrusto, I know you loved my grandmother, and I appreciated that. Rest in peace."

As Dario looked closer at Hrusto's headstone, he saw the German phrase 'the treasure you seek will be found after you die' etched in the stone.

"That's interesting. That's the same saying that's on my grandmother's ring," Dario said.

Dario picked up the flower receptacle and forced it back into the ground. As he did, he heard the base of the metal flower receptacle hit something hard. He pulled out the receptacle, looked in the hole, and saw something shiny that looked like gold.

The Picture Box

"The treasure I seek?" Dario said to himself.

THE END

www.ingramcontent.com/pod-product-compliance
Lightning Source LLC
LaVergne TN
LVHW040157080526
838202LV00042B/3193